Misty Point

Also by Linda Rawlins

Misty Point Mystery Series:
Misty Manor
Misty Point

Rocky Meadow Mystery Series:
The Bench
Fatal Breach
Sacred Gold

Misty Point

Linda Rawlins
Riverbench Publishing, LLC

Misty Point
By
Linda Rawlins

Copyright © 2017 by Linda Rawlins

ISBN-13
EBook: 978-0-9914230-4-0
Softcover: 978-0-9914230-3-3

Discover other titles by Linda Rawlins at
www.lindarawlins.com

Dedicated to my mom.
Also known as Joycie, Gma, J.

For
Giving me the love of reading as a child.
The literal tools to write.
Being one of my greatest cheerleaders.
Being my initial editor.
Quoting Ernest Hemingway to me while sitting in a pub for hours on end, while I edit.
And for her famous words of wisdom
"Just write, dammit."

Acknowledgements

It takes a village to raise an author – I expressed that thought at a recent SinC meeting. One can write a story but it takes a fantastic team to turn it into a book. I have a special team who helps to reshape, refine, polish and help me publish!

Krista Liotti – My special content editor and social media manager who takes my initial manuscript and gives me the honest feedback I need to refine my efforts. She rocks and I Thank you!!

Matt Liotti – Fantastic producer who does my covers, formatting, social media sites, website, banners, and everything else necessary to support my efforts and platform. Without him, my manuscript would hardly get off the ground! He is great and can be found at www.riverbenchpublishing.com

Joe Liotti - Special thanks to my husband Joe for holding everything else together while we publish.

My First Readers Club – Special thanks to Sandi Chapin, Krista O'Neill, Anita Uotinen, Lorraine Rawlins, Zelda Feigen, Joseph Liotti, Joyce Rawlins, Claire Liotti – your support, feedback and corrections are invaluable!

Final Read – A special thanks to Lori Krempa for the final proofread!! She caught many we missed and was kind enough to neglect sleep and push forward through the deadlines. I am forever grateful!!

Once again, I am grateful to my readers for enjoying my books and for coming out to support me at all author events. Thank you!!

There is nothing to writing. All you do is sit down at a typewriter and bleed – Ernest Hemingway

Happy Reading!

Chapter One

"We're almost done," he whispered softly.

"I hope so." Megan sighed as she placed the Mont Blanc pen on the mahogany desk and rubbed her right temple. She procrastinated by looking around the formal library of Misty Manor.

He picked up the pen and pressed it back into Megan's hand. "Please, we only have two more signatures and it's important."

"Wait a minute. I think I'm starting to have a panic attack," Megan said, rubbing the back of her neck with her opposite hand.

"Take a deep breath so we can finish." After waiting a few seconds, Teddy pointed to two lines on the paper. "Now, please sign here and here."

Megan swallowed, leaned forward and scribbled her name. "There, I'm done." She dropped the five-hundred-dollar pen on the desk as Teddy picked up and straightened the pile of papers before he handed them to the notary sitting quietly on the side.

"Excellent, I'll have these filed immediately." Teddy smiled as he collected his pen, opened his briefcase and placed several folders inside.

"Everything is happening so fast," Megan pleaded.

Teddy stopped what he was doing and sat down on the opposite side of the desk. "Megan, please trust me. In another three days, you can consult any accountant or attorney you'd like, but give me the benefit of the doubt."

"It has nothing to do with trust," Megan said, feeling guilty. "You've been legal counsel for Grandma Rose for decades and I'm sure you would do anything to make sure her wishes were carried out." Megan paused again and looked around the dark, gloomy room which matched her mood perfectly. "But, I have no clue what's going on."

"I know, but you will. And yes, I'd do anything to follow your grandmother's wishes. You know how close I was to Rose. She was like a mother to me." Teddy grimaced at the memory of her death, as he reached across the desk and squeezed Megan's hand.

"I'm her granddaughter and I want to see her wishes carried out as well, but I'm not the woman she was," Megan said, shrugging her shoulders as she offered a sad smile.

"Rose was a brilliant woman and I have faith she knew what she was doing. We can discuss the situation after the weekend, but I'm going to file everything today. I need three days. Time is of the essence."

Megan sighed. "Teddy, I'm scared. Don't you get that? My great-grandparents built Misty Manor and developed a town around it. Grandma Rose grew Misty Point to be a fantastic beach community. Many people live here and depended on her. I don't want to be the Stanford who fails the town."

"Just the opposite, my dear. Your grandmother knew how much you love Misty Manor and Misty Point. She knew you wouldn't sell the town or its citizens short."

"But…," Megan started.

Teddy held his hand up. "No buts, and before you say something negative, which will annoy me, Rose arranged everything for you. Please don't suggest she had a selfish reason for planning her estate the way she did."

"I don't know the first thing about running a business, much less a town," Megan shouted in frustration. She balled her hands into fists and hit the desk.

"Nevertheless, in a few days, you'll be a powerful woman in Misty Point, if not in the county or state. Your holdings will be vast and varied. You'll be asked to serve as board chair for many committees and will be addressed as such."

"That's exactly my point," Megan said. "What do I know about being a board chair?"

Teddy chuckled. "What gives you the impression anyone on a board or committee knows what they're doing?"

Megan considered his eyes and shrugged.

"Some members know exactly what they're doing and are very good at it. Others have zero knowledge of law, politics or civility, but they have money. Do you know what some of the best committee members bring to the table?"

Megan shook her head. "Like I said, no clue."

Teddy stood up and smiled. He placed his hands on the desk and leaned toward her. "Passion, Megan. That's right, passion. The best members bring intense enthusiasm and an unstoppable energy to make things happen. Let the lawyers and accountants sweat the details. Rose always did, but she knew what she wanted to accomplish and wouldn't let anyone get in her way."

"That's the point. I have no clue what I want and I'm ashamed to admit I don't know what Rose wanted," Megan said as she choked up. "I lost track of her passions when I left Misty Manor." Megan stood and walked toward the window where a steady torrent of rain beat against the glass. A sudden flash of lightning, followed by a thunderous boom, made everyone jump.

Teddy began to laugh. "It's just like your grandmother to put her two cents in the conversation."

Megan sniffed as she watched the rain. She moved the heavy damask curtains and peered out toward the beach. "Damn this rain. The weather station predicted heavy storms all week."

"I've heard. The surf has been rough the last couple of days with several tropical storms off the coast," Teddy said. "Five foot waves and you can barely see the jetties. But with all things, there's an ebb and flow. The storms will calm down."

Megan smiled as she turned. "Apparently, the weather matches my mood."

"Nonsense," Teddy said as he waived his hand in her direction. "You're grieving, going through a flood of emotions, which is perfectly normal. Give yourself time. Losing someone you love is one of the most difficult things to endure." Teddy smiled as he looked at her. She was a medium height with light brown hair and bags under her eyes. Megan looked just like Rose when they first met. "Don't worry. When you're ready, I have someone to help you navigate the boardrooms and committees." Teddy walked over to Megan and offered a fatherly embrace. "We'll talk again next week. Try to relax and catch up on your sleep."

Megan nodded and let out a heavy sigh. "You're right. I haven't been sleeping well."

"How could you? You've had quite an adventure since returning to New Jersey, uncovering a big family secret. Most people come to the shore to relax and enjoy the ocean, but you were always independent." Teddy smiled as he shook his head. "You need time to rest and recover. We'll get everything straightened out eventually, but we made big strides today."

"Yes, big strides," Megan repeated in a defeated tone as her shoulders dropped.

Teddy picked up his briefcase. "Walk me to the front door." He turned and nodded at Ellen, his notary and secretary. "We have quite a few stops to make this afternoon. We'd better get started."

The small group entered the foyer but stopped when they heard pounding on the front door.

Megan jumped and let out a nervous laugh.

"I don't think it's the bogeyman," Teddy said as he placed a reassuring hand on her shoulder. "Relax."

"Who could it be?" Megan asked, perplexed. "I'm not expecting anyone except Marie and that's not until tomorrow."

Lightning continued to flash as rain pounded the porch. Someone jiggled the front doorknob and shouted outside.

Teddy shifted his briefcase. "Whoever it is, he doesn't sound happy. We'd better check it out." He crossed the remaining distance of the foyer and turned the lock. Pulling the knob, he opened the door a few inches and peered outside.

Two men stood in the pouring rain. The ocean wind blew gusts of water inside the entrance hall.

"Stand back, we need to get the hell inside." The two men picked up their luggage and quickly crossed the threshold. One of them turned and said, "Teddy, close the damn door."

Teddy did as he was instructed, effectively blocking any further rain from blowing into the house.

The stranger brushed water from his shirt as a small puddle gathered around his feet. "Damn, this is a Givenchy polo shirt." He then turned toward Megan and said, "Holy cow, look at you."

Megan's eyes widened and her mouth dropped open. "Dad?"

"The one and only, darling," he said with a laugh. "You look great."

Megan's eyes flashed as she stared at her father, Dean. "What are you doing here?"

"Is that any way to greet your father? Come here, give me a hug." Dean held his arms open as he stepped toward his daughter.

Megan jumped backward and held her hand up. "Are you kidding me? As far as I'm concerned, you can drop dead." Megan's hands shook as her heart hammered in her throat.

"Well that didn't go the way I imagined," Dean said, with a laugh. Megan continued to glare as he turned to introduce his guest. "I want you all to meet my friend, Randall Douglas. He's from Texas and wants to see the Jersey Shore." The group remained silent so Dean pressed on. "Randall, this is my daughter, Megan Stanford."

The man plucked the Stetson off his head, smiled and said, "Howdy, ma'am."

Megan gave a curt nod, but remained silent.

"And this is my mother's attorney, Theodore Harrison Carter," Dean said as he introduced his friend. "We call him Teddy."

Randall Douglas reached out and shook Teddy's hand. "Glad to meet ya'," he said with a smile.

Teddy nodded. "My pleasure."

Dean clapped Teddy on the back. "It's good to see you. I guess we have a lot to talk about."

Teddy pressed a tight smile, but not before Megan notice him stiffen. "Actually, Ellen and I were just leaving for a meeting downtown. Perhaps, another day." He turned toward his trusted notary and held out his hand. "We'll have to hurry in this rain, but I don't want either of us to slip."

"Yes, of course," Ellen said in a nervous voice as she hurried to the door. "Very nice to meet you all."

Teddy opened the door, looked outside and turned back toward Ellen. "Ready?" When she nodded, he opened the door wide, popped open his umbrella and shielded them both as they hurried out to the waiting Mercedes Benz. The remaining group watched from the foyer before closing the door to keep out the rain.

"It's a shame they had to leave right away," Dean said. "I have to talk to him." Turning back to Megan, he said, "Hey, you have anything to drink around here?"

Megan was silent for a moment, then shrugged. "There's some iced tea in the fridge."

Dean laughed. "I was thinking of something with a bit more charge."

"Sorry, no alcohol here." Megan said sarcastically. "I haven't had time to shop. I've been busy since I returned home."

"Yes, I heard," Dean said as he whistled. "A diamond necklace? Wow."

"I was talking about taking care of Grandma Rose," Megan said, stiffly. "Who, by the way, is now in her final resting place with Grandpa George."

"Yes, I'm so sorry I couldn't make it back from Europe," Dean said, shaking his head to show remorse, but failing miserably. "I had several important business commitments." Dean nodded toward Randall.

Megan paused for a moment to take a calming breath so she wouldn't scream. "I see. And how is Gigi?"

Dean shrugged. "Sadly, her opening did not fare well. She decided to spend some time in Geneva, Switzerland, with her mother."

Gritting her teeth, Megan plastered a polite smile on her face. "Sorry to hear."

"I would have gone with her, but when I got word from Randall he'd be free to visit Misty Manor, I rushed back as soon as I could."

Megan struggled to swallow and remain quiet while in the presence of Randall Douglas. She didn't know who he was or how he knew her father, but Megan knew she'd have some very choice words for Dean when they were alone.

"Hey, I told Randall we have plenty of rooms in Misty Manor and we're both hungry. So, what do you have?"

Megan stared at him for a moment while keeping her arms crossed. "What I have is plenty of rooms which have been unused for years. There are clean sheets in the pantry and towels in the bathroom. In the kitchen, you'll find two cans of tuna fish and half of a banana on the counter. Please feel free to help yourself."

Dean turned and looked at Randall. "We may have a little work to do. Let me show you around. Hopefully, the rain will stop, then we can go out and get a steak."

"Can't wait," Randall said as he tapped his belly, hidden under a designer Ralph Lauren Suit. "Quite frankly, I'm starving."

Dean turned back to his daughter. "Where's the best place to get a steak around here? It would help if they had an expensive Remy Martin cognac for afterward." Dean chuckled as he looked at Randall for confirmation.

"Gee, Dad," Megan said, while posing with her best thinking face. "I haven't been able to afford much more than Antonio's pizza, but if you really want cognac, try the Portside. I hear it's quite the place these days."

Not acknowledging the sarcasm, Dean said, "That sounds perfect. Where is it?"

Megan shook her head. "It's on 8th, near the marina. I don't know if you need reservations. Perhaps, you should call."

Dean laughed and turned back to his friend. "We know how to handle reservations, don't we, Randall?" Dean walked over, guffawed and threw his arm around Randall's shoulders. "C'mon, let's go for a tour. I think you're gonna love Misty Manor."

Chapter Two

Once the two men left the foyer, Megan noticed her hands were shaking. She was close to tears and still had a small headache playing around her right temple. The day had been stressful enough with the anticipation of meeting Teddy. Signing legal papers was not her idea of an ideal afternoon. Having her father waltz in with a friend was insulting. He was too busy to return home to take care of Grandma Rose while she was on hospice, too busy to attend the funeral, but apparently had plenty of time to arrange for steaks and expensive brandy.

Megan turned and hurried up the grand staircase. Instead of climbing the next flight to her room, she chose to go to her grandmother's room. Megan opened the door, turned on the dim light and walked inside. Her grandmother's bed was made up with her favorite teal blue duvet set. The high thread count allowed the sheets and bedding to be extremely soft and welcoming.

Photos of Megan's grandparents were displayed on the mahogany end table situated next to the bed. There were various photos of Rose and George in their youth, as well as their wedding photo. Her grandmother's favorite Queen Anne chair, covered in peach damask, sat next to the end table. Across the room, the window framed an early evening view of the ocean. Dark clouds gathered in the distance and threw lightning bolts from the sky toward the water.

Megan's heart grabbed as she looked around the room. Grandma Rose died three weeks ago. Megan was trying to heal, to process her grief, as well as her guilt and move on. On her worst days, she would come to her grandmother's room, lie on the soft bed and recall the best moments of their relationship.

Megan felt a vibration in her back pocket. She brushed a tear from her cheek and pulled out her cell phone. She hit the green button and answered with a nasal voice. "Hello?"

"Megan, it's Teddy. Are you alone?"

"Yes, as far as I know. Why?" Megan asked as she looked around.

"I wanted to warn you but I couldn't say anything before I left."

"Warn me about what?" Megan asked, confused.

"Your father," Teddy whispered. "He doesn't know, yet."

"Apparently, I don't know, either. What are you talking about?"

Teddy sighed. "The estate, of course. Do not discuss your grandmother's estate with your father or his friend. Do not agree to anything they may ask of you. Do not sign anything. Do not talk about Misty Manor or any of your grandmother's assets and most importantly, keep her room, her office, and the attic locked."

"Teddy?"

"Listen, I have to go. I will purposely be away for the weekend and I will not meet or talk to your father until next week. If he asks you anything, or tries to arrange anything, tell him he must talk to me first. Understand?"

"I think so, and it won't be hard, because I don't know exactly what's going on," Megan whispered into the phone.

"It's better that way. I'll talk to you next week. Don't call me unless it's an emergency," Teddy said before he hung up his phone.

Confused, Megan shook her head and left her grandmother's room. She closed the door behind her and realized she wasn't sure if there was a key. The door remained unlocked when Grandma Rose was ill so she could receive immediate help, if necessary. Megan made a mental note to search for a key as soon as she could.

Walking down the hall, Megan was stopped by her father as she crossed the landing to the grand staircase.

"There you are," Dean said. "I've been looking for you."

"Well, evidently you found me," Megan said sarcastically as her stomach clenched. "You must need something."

"No need to be a witch," Dean said without a smile. "The rain has slowed down and considering the lack of clean beds and sheets in Misty Manor, Randall and I will be going to Atlantic City for the weekend."

"Excellent," Megan said, a feeling of relief settling inside her chest.

"But, we'll be back Sunday afternoon," Dean said with a scowl. "It's very important Randall Douglas be impressed with Misty Manor, as well as the rest of town."

Megan felt a sense of dread begin to suffocate her breathing once again. "Why is that?"

Dean shook his head and lowered his voice. "I can't talk about anything right now. While we're gone, I want you to get help, some local college kids or something and clean this place up. It's a mess."

"What should I do? Offer them hot chocolate and cookies for their labor?" Megan asked sarcastically.

"You had Marie working here when Rose was dying. Get her back. Freshen up the place. Open the windows, get rid of the dust and liven things up."

Megan took a deep quiet breath, crossed her arms and clenched her jaw. "I came back here to take care of Grandma, not work as your servant."

Dean grabbed and squeezed her arm. "Megan, if you screw this up for me, I swear...," Dean turned red when Megan cut him off.

"What Dad? You'll send me to bed without supper? Beat me?" She stared down at his hand on her arm.

Dean's face turned an angry purple as the veins in his neck starting pulsing. "You just wait and see."

"Dean, are you up there?" The terse voice of Randall Douglas floated upstairs. "The car is here. I've got my luggage ready to go. Are you coming?"

Dean Stanford took a deep breath, released Megan's arm and turned toward the foyer. "Coming, be down in a minute. Just saying goodbye to my beautiful daughter."

"Ok, but hurry up, will you? I've got a juicy steak with my name on it waiting in Atlantic City."

Dean turned back to Megan and pointed a finger in her face. "Sunday afternoon. This place better be clean, got it?" He then turned, ran down the stairs and clapped Randall on the back. "Ready to go? This trip is going to be great."

Megan stood at the top of the stairs, rubbing her arm until she heard the front door close. Tears slid down her face as she whispered. "Goodbye, Dad. Great to see you, too. No, I didn't mind being here all alone while Grandma Rose was dying. And yes, I missed you too."

Chapter Three

Megan walked to her room and sat on the bed. She was tired, emotional, depressed and in the perfect mood for a pity party. It was Friday night and she had received multiple calls to go out with the gang for pizza and drinks. Nick, Georgie, Amber and Tommy had been trying to get her to leave the house since Grandma Rose died. As much as she loved her friends, she simply couldn't bring herself to relax and laugh.

Signing legal papers with Teddy and seeing her deadbeat father made things a lot worse. Megan flopped back onto the bed, her head landing on the soft pillow. The air conditioner helped process a cloud of humidity, the likes of which was typically found in the islands. The room was dark and as she closed her eyes, Megan could hardly believe she'd only been back in New Jersey for ten weeks. She hadn't had time to catch her breath and needed a few weeks to sleep and breathe. She missed her grandmother and needed time to emotionally deal with everything. Losing her job and then Grandma Rose was a lot to process. There was very little money left in her savings. Initially, the attorney offered to give her money to buy food and pay bills, but she declined out of pride. Her father's demands notwithstanding, she may have no choice but to accept help from Teddy when she saw him again.

Megan kept her eyes closed while her mind whirled. The last thing she remembered before drifting off to sleep was saying a little prayer Grandma Rose taught her to say as a child when she was worried.

When it's dark and I can't see
Please, Lord, take good care of me
In the morning, when the sun is new
I promise Lord, I'll pray for you

Chapter Four

"Nick, you're going to have to drag her out of the house," Georgie said as she passed a chili cheese dog over the table. "She needs an intervention."

"I've been calling," Nick said as he pulled five or six napkins out of the dingy, black napkin holder. "She keeps putting me off. I'm trying to respect her privacy and I know she needs to work through her grandmother's death, but I think you're right."

"Hey, save me a French fry," Amber said as she stared at the red and white checkered paper boat holding a pile of hot steaming fries.

Georgie turned toward her friend with eyebrows raised. Laughing she said, "Well, since I know you'll only eat one, why don't you pick out your choice fry?"

"You're a toad," Amber said, making a face.

"C'mon, stop fooling around," Tommy said. "What should we do about Megan?"

"Didn't the hospice say someone from bereavement would reach out to her? Do you think she ever talked to them?" Georgie asked the group.

"No idea," Nick said as he stuffed the last of his onion rings in his mouth. He looked at his watch. "It's too late to go storming over there now but I'm going to Misty Manor in the morning. Who's with me?" He looked around the table at quiet faces. "What?"

Georgie grimaced and took the lead. "Nick, it would be awkward for all of us to show up at once. Why don't you go over in the morning and get her out of the house? Walk on the beach, take her for breakfast, whatever it takes. If it works, we could all meet you somewhere or arrange dinner or whatever she wants."

"You know, keep it subtle," Tommy said. "I've got free time during the day tomorrow, but Tommy and the Tides are booked to play the Arena tomorrow night."

"I don't know if she's ready for that," Nick said thoughtfully. "Amber, are you going to watch Tommy or are you free tomorrow night?"

"If Megan agrees to do something, I'll be with her. Otherwise, I'll go watch Tommy."

"We could have a bonfire on the beach," Georgie suggested. "Something quiet but supportive. You know, get her mind off the last two months."

"Okay, I'll go over in the morning," Nick said, wiping his mouth. "But, I may need help so stay close to your phones."

"Will do," Georgie said. "Let us know if she wants to do something later in the day."

"You can bet I'll be in touch," Nick said finishing his drink.

Chapter Five

Megan rolled over and pulled the duvet up to her chin. She curled into a fetal position and drifted off to sleep for another half hour, but woke as the sun began to pierce her eyelids. Initially, she tossed and turned with stress dreams about her father, Grandma Rose and Misty Manor until she fell into a deep sleep early in the morning.

Feeling more rested than she expected, Megan rose from bed and dressed in her favorite shorts and t-shirt. She ran a brush through her hair and headed down the hall with thoughts of rich, dark coffee. She descended the stairs to the second floor and decided to stop in her grandmother's room, while she was alone, to make sure it was secure.

Crossing the threshold, her heart gave a quick squeeze when she saw the beautiful things which provided so much joy to her grandmother. Not necessarily expensive, they were mementos collected over the years and connected to special memories. A shared favorite was an old glass baby food jar which held all the sea glass they had collected from the beach when she was young.

After letting her mind get lost in memories of shimmering glass, Megan remembered she was there to look for a key to Grandma Rose's room. But, what was Teddy so afraid of that it had to be locked?

Megan spent several moments searching the dresser and the items stored on the top. Up until now, she hadn't been able to bring herself to go through Rose's things, but Teddy said it was important. In one of the drawers, she found a trinket box behind some scarves. Megan slowly opened the box and found a beautiful pair of emerald earrings, several rusted safety pins, a few loose pennies and the key to the bedroom door. She couldn't resist taking a few minutes to hold her grandmother's scarves and breathe in the lingering scent of her favorite perfume.

Realizing she was getting upset, she replaced the scarves and pushed the drawer closed. Megan crossed the room and stepped into the hallway. She pulled the door closed and secured it with the key.

Slipping it into her pocket, she headed down the grand staircase and into the foyer. As she passed her grandmother's office, she realized she would have to start going through the books and finances soon. Bills were piling up from utilities, insurance companies and the town. Megan dreaded having to close each account while providing documentation Rose had passed, but it had to be done.

Heeding Teddy's advice, she entered the office and opened the desk drawer. She pawed through pens, pencils, rubber bands and paper clips. Grabbing the ring of keys located on the side, she picked them up and took a moment to look around the small room.

Despite the fact Grandma Rose was a prominent woman in town, involved in many committees and businesses, her office displayed the same humble demeanor as her personality. Megan looked at her grandmother's desk and tried to envision her working there before the illness took over.

A wave of sadness washed over Megan, as she realized she might never be as astute and bright as her grandmother was, especially while working in this very room. She would have to start pawing through the mounds of paper and attend to her affairs, but she simply wasn't ready. She could afford to wait another week which would give her time to talk to Teddy again.

In the meantime, she would follow his advice. She stepped away from the desk, pushing the antique-crafted wooden chair underneath, and slowly padded out of the room, but not before she made sure to lock the door and slip yet another key ring into the pocket of her jeans.

As she continued toward the kitchen in the back of the house, she heard a persistent knocking at the front door. Not expecting anyone, her shoulders slumped in anticipation her father and his friend had returned unexpectedly from Atlantic City.

Megan crossed the foyer to the front door and peered through the peep hole. No one stood in front of the door, but on the porch, near the top step, she spied a beautiful bouquet of flowers. She strained to look to the sides of the porch and saw no one so she opened the front door and stepped outside.

Puzzled as to whom would leave flowers, she crossed to the bouquet and picked it up. Megan took a moment to smell the beautiful fragrance of the delicately balanced array of blooms before she began to search for a card. She was so distracted, she didn't notice someone else was on the porch until he wrapped muscled arms around her.

Chapter Six

Yelling out, Megan dropped the flowers and stiffened.

"Hey, Megan, it's just me," Nick said as he turned her to face him. He had a big smile on his face. "What's up?"

Megan looked up at him with tears in her eyes as she trembled. "That wasn't funny, Nick. You scared me."

He wrapped his strong, tanned arms around her once more and hugged her to his tight body. Whispering in her ear, he said, "I'm sorry, that certainly was not my intent."

"Then why did you leave the flowers on the porch and hide?" Megan said, looking up at him.

Nick looked down at her. He kissed her on the nose and said, "To be honest, I wanted to make sure you came outside. I want to take you to breakfast. I miss hugging you, messing up your hair and talking. You've been locked up in the house for weeks since Rose died and it's not healthy." Nick took a step back and picked up the bouquet of flowers from the floor. He adjusted them and properly handed them to Megan with a bow. "I apologize, will you please have breakfast with me?"

Megan paused for a few seconds, struggling with decision. Nick looked so damn cute this morning. He was one of the finest police officers Misty Point employed and they had grown up together. In high school, he asked her to prom and she refused him. A year later, they both graduated and she left town to attend college and begin a career as a journalist for a virtual newspaper in Detroit. She never realized she had broken his heart until she returned to New Jersey a few months ago to take care of her dying grandmother. In the interim, he had matured into quite a handsome man.

"I was about to make a pot of coffee." Megan said, pointing to the front door.

"No, I want you to leave the house. Let's go to Stanley's for a bagel sandwich. We can argue over whether we want to order Taylor

Ham or pork roll." Nick laughed as he gave her another hug. "It's so good to see you again."

Megan ran her fingers through her hair. "Okay, I have to get my purse."

"You look great," Nick said, as he saw her indecision. "Fine, get your purse, but if you back out, I'll have no choice but to arrest you."

Megan laughed, for the first time in a while. "For what?"

"I'll think of something," he said as he grinned from ear to ear. "Of course, I'll have to think of a proper sentence, too."

Megan blushed in response. "Let's just get the purse."

They went inside the house and Megan scurried toward the kitchen. "Nick, I want to put the flowers in a vase before we leave."

Nick followed her into the kitchen and watched as she cut the stems to allow them to draw as much fresh water as possible. Her hair hung over a portion of her face and although she looked tired and stressed, her beauty still radiated underneath.

Megan turned and placed the magnificent arrangement on the kitchen table and smiled.

"Don't look now, but I think you're actually smiling," he pointed out.

"The flowers are beautiful," Megan said as she looked up at him. "Thank you."

"Thank me later, let's go eat. I'm starving," Nick said as he extended his hand to her.

Chapter Seven

Megan watched the ocean roll by as the breeze danced through her hair. She looked over at Nick. He looked great behind the wheel of his Camaro. Not in uniform, he was wearing pressed jeans and a tight sapphire blue t-shirt. He was freshly shaved and his end of summer, well-tanned, muscled arms looked fantastic as he pressed them against the steering wheel. Megan enjoyed the mingling scents of the briny ocean and his cologne as the warm breeze flowed over her. For the first time in weeks she felt herself relax as she melted into the seat behind her.

Nick looked at Megan and smiled. "See, there's life outside the walls of Misty Manor."

"I see that," Megan said as she reached out and touched his arm. "It's been a tough few weeks for me."

"It's been almost four weeks to be exact," Nick said. "Your friends were planning on storming the castle if you didn't come out with me this morning. They said they've been calling and dropping by but they haven't been able to reach you."

"Who exactly is they?" Megan asked, sadness etched on her face.

"Georgie, Amber, Tommy, me," Nick said as he slowed the car on Main Street. "Hell, Tommy's entire band has been asking if you're okay." Nick pulled to the curb in front on Stanley's Bagels. "Can you believe this? It's the middle of August and we got a parking spot right in front of Stanley's."

Megan shook her head. "I can't believe it's August already. The last couple of months have flown by. I feel like I just got here to take care of Rose and she's already gone." Megan's lip trembled as her eyes filled with tears. She quickly checked her pockets for a tissue. Within seconds, Nick pulled out his handkerchief and thrust it under her nose.

"Megan, you're grieving. I get that and I'm certainly not going to tell you how you should feel. I just wish you'd let your friends support you more. We all loved Rose and she meant a lot to us and the whole town. I'm sure there are many ways we can memorialize her. Maybe we can all work on a project together."

Megan looked at Nick as he dried her tears. "I hadn't really thought about that. What do you think we should do? A scholarship to college?"

Nick stuffed his handkerchief back in his pocket and mussed Megan's hair. "Knowing all the committees and boards she was on, I think you'll be deluged with plaques and dedications once you get out there, which you need to do soon. Isn't there a bereavement department or something at Cape Shore Hospice? They can help you too."

Megan looked through the windshield and sighed deeply. "Someone left a couple of messages and sent a letter or two, but I haven't answered them."

"Maybe you should think about it," Nick said as he massaged the back of her neck. Megan turned toward him with a small smile and was rewarded with a kiss on the cheek. "Now, let's go. I'm starving and I don't want to have to wait in line."

Nick opened his door and popped out of the car while Megan did the same on her side. Nick circled the car, grabbed her by the hand and led her inside Stanley's. The two grabbed a table in the back and within a few minutes had ordered drinks and their sandwiches. As the waitress walked away, Megan said, "These college kids look younger every year."

Nick laughed. "I know." He pointed to a flyer on the wall. "Looks like Stanley is already advertising for help. I imagine most of the college kids will be moving back to their dorms in a couple of weeks."

Megan laughed. "Oh, so many memories."

"Do tell," Nick said as he leaned back in his chair and crossed his arms.

Megan blushed and shook her head. "Not today, my friend. It's interesting when you look back on college with a fondness that may not have existed while you were living through the actual experience."

"That's true." Nick leaned out of the way as their food was delivered to the table. He continued to make small talk as Megan checked her coffee. "I see you like cream. I usually like my coffee black." When Megan didn't answer, he tried again. "Shall we actually discuss the philosophical differences between Taylor Ham and pork roll?"

Megan smiled and took a big sip of her latte. "Not necessary at the moment." The sandwich and coffee tasted delicious as she realized how many meals she had skipped over the last couple of weeks.

"So how are things?" Nick asked. "I drove by yesterday and there were cars in the driveway. Did you have company?"

Megan blanched and swallowed hard. She put the uneaten part of her sandwich back on the plate and sat back in her seat. Looking at Nick, she said, "You're never going to believe who showed up yesterday."

"Santa Claus? Bruce Springsteen?"

Megan smiled and shook her head.

"Wait, don't tell me. Elvis? Right? Am I right?" Nick teased as he spread his arms.

"I wish it were any one of them," Megan said. "But, no. Can you believe my dear father showed up with a friend in tow?"

"Get out," Nick said, genuinely surprised. "Who was with him, Gigi?"

Megan laughed out loud. "Oh, no. Gigi flew off to another country but I'm sure he has her on speed dial." Megan shrugged. "Unless she ran out of money."

Nick would have laughed, but didn't out of respect for Megan. He swallowed his food, took a drink and reached out for her hand. "Okay, then who was with him."

"A gentleman from Texas."

"So, let me get this straight," Nick said, beginning to get agitated. "He couldn't bother to break away from Gigi long enough to come to his own mother's funeral or even send flowers but several weeks later he nonchalantly shows up with some guy in tow."

"You got it," Megan said angrily as she nodded her head.

"Megan, no disrespect to you or your family but it's obvious your father has an agenda to fulfill. He isn't here because he missed the place."

"That's what hurts so much." Megan swallowed hard as she wiped away tears with the palm of her hand and looked down at the table. "I'm so upset, Nick."

"I'm sorry, Megan. You dad is a conceited jerk. You deserve to be upset."

"Instead of being sad about his mother, he was angry when he wasn't with his friend. He frightened me."

"How? Did you feel threatened in any way?" Nick asked, feeling protective.

Instinctively, Megan began to rub her arm and Nick noted the bruises which had formed there. "Did he do that to you?"

"What?" Megan asked.

"Your arm. How did you get those bruises?"

"Oh, yeah. My dad grabbed my arm but I don't think he meant to hurt me."

Nick swallowed hard, clenched his teeth and kept his mouth shut. He couldn't possibly voice his thoughts without upsetting Megan more than she already was. After a few moments, Nick picked up his sandwich and took a bite. He chewed thoroughly and swallowed hoping he would calm down. "Are they at the house now?"

"Who?" Megan asked, sipping at her latte.

"Your father and his friend."

"No, they weren't happy I couldn't provide warm fluffy beds, a tender steak and expensive cognac so they left to spend the rest of the weekend in Atlantic City." Megan started laughing inappropriately at her own statement. "Can you believe it? I barely have enough in my savings to buy food next week and his concern is wining and dining some stranger."

Nick put his sandwich down and reached across the table to take Megan's hand in his. "You'll never be without the things you need to be comfortable. Megan, you have a lot of friends and if I ever find out you aren't eating or doing anything for lack of money, I'll go nuts. Let me help you," Nick said as he willed her to be less stoic.

Megan wiped at her nose. "Nick, thank you but I'm fine. It's frustrating because my father is all over himself with this guy and Teddy has not officially held a reading of my grandmother's will. Regardless of what the endpoint is, it's all rather crass."

"I still don't like it," Nick said as he let go of her arm.

"Teddy told me I have a little money coming my way, so I'll be okay. I'm sure he'll be able to advance something for me." Megan pulled a paper napkin from the dispenser and blew her nose. "See, that's why I didn't want to talk about it. I can't even think of her without crying."

Nick smiled. "I believe it's called grieving. From what I was told in training, you can't go around it and you can't will it away. You have to go through it. It's painful, but ultimately necessary for you to move on with your life. Go ahead and cry. I'll just finish my sandwich if you don't mind."

Megan couldn't hold back a laugh. She balled up the napkin and threw it at him. Without hesitation, he redirected it as he chewed. Once he swallowed, he pointed to her food and said, "Hey, the least you can do is finish your breakfast."

Megan looked down at her plate. She admitted she was still hungry and bit into her sandwich. The two spent the next couple minutes eating as they held hands. When she was done, Megan took another napkin and wiped her mouth. "Thank you. I can't believe how hungry I was."

"That's what happens when you don't eat regularly," Nick teased as he pushed his plate to the side. He looked up at Megan and became serious. "I don't want to drag the mood down but do you have any idea what your father's end game may be?"

Megan slowly shook her head. "I don't. To be honest, he probably wants exactly what everyone is expecting from him. He did tell me it was extremely important Mr. Douglas liked Misty Manor, so I'm sure my father wants him to put in an offer."

"Mr. Douglas?" Nick asked.

"Yes, that was his name, Randall Douglas from Texas," Megan confirmed.

Nick nodded. "Got it, maybe I can do a little research on Randall Douglas from Texas."

"He looked like he was comfortable around money," Megan said.

"Can your father do that?" Nick asked.

"Do what?"

"Can he start showing off the place?"

"I don't know," Megan said. "I'm not sure who inherits. Teddy was with me when they arrived and he blew my father off, even though it was obvious my father wanted to speak to him."

Nick sat back in his chair. "Is that so?"

"Yes, and then Teddy called me ten minutes later and made me promise not to sign or agree to anything my father said, so he must suspect my father's ulterior motives as well."

"I don't think that's a stretch. The whole town thinks the same."

"Nick," Megan paused and swallowed. "You won't tell anyone the things I'm telling you, right?"

A funny expression crossed Nick's face as he listened to her question. "Why would I do that?"

"I don't know and I don't mean to insult you because I know you're trying to help me, but you're very dedicated to Misty Point. I know a lot of people feel strongly about the future of the town and wouldn't hesitate to put their two cents in, if given the opportunity."

Nick looked down at the table for a moment and then back at Megan. "It's true I love Misty Point. I've lived here my whole life. I've sworn to protect the town and its residents and I hope to stay here a very long time, but to be honest, my first concern is you. I would not repeat any confidential information, ever. To be honest, I will have a problem if I ever see your father lay a hand on you."

Megan felt herself blushing as Nick spoke.

"I like you Megan, very much. I'm sorry the circumstances that brought us back together are not ideal, but time passes. And yes, people are very jittery right now, because they don't know what will happen once your grandmother's property changes hands. But, I promise you, my devotion is to you. I wouldn't tell anyone your business."

Megan seemed satisfied and nodded. "I didn't realize how wealthy Rose was and I still don't know the total worth of her estate. Once Teddy gives us a formal reading, we'll know exactly who got what and go from there."

Nick nodded. "Fair enough."

"For the record, it breaks my heart to think my father would be here just to scavenge her estate. He's no better than a vulture."

"Or a shark," Nick added. "Or a seagull. Did you know seagulls eat carrion when they can't find fresh food?"

Megan looked up at him and laughed again. "Thanks, I'm trying to have a philosophical moment, and you're worried about seagull food but I appreciate you validating my feelings."

"Not a problem," Nick said, grinning ear to ear. "I help my own."

The two were interrupted by their server asking if they were interested in anything else. Nick paid the bill, took Megan by the arm and escorted her to the car. After opening the car door, he kissed her on the cheek and whispered in her ear. "Did I tell you how great it is to see you laugh again?"

Chapter Eight

"You didn't have to do that," Megan said as they whipped down Ocean Ave. The car windows were wide open and the salty breeze smelled great.

"Do what?" Nick asked, feigning ignorance.

Megan punched his arm. "You didn't have to buy all those groceries for me."

"I didn't buy them for you." Nick smiled which caused Megan to feel herself melt in response. "Seriously, I bought them for me. I plan on spending a lot of time at Misty Manor and I need more than an old can of tuna fish."

Megan was pleased to hear Nick wanted to spend more time with her. She was tired of being sad and lonely. To hide her expression, she turned toward the beach. "Wow, the surf is pretty rough."

"Yeah, those tropical storms are stirring everything up. Waves are up to six feet with a heavy undertow."

Megan stared at the water crashing on the beach. The rain had stopped but the sky remained dark. The waves were powerful and dangerous and equally exhilarating to watch. "Plenty of surfers paddling out there."

"I'm sure. They're always hunting for the biggest wave," Nick said. "Thankfully, the lightning has stopped."

Nick reached the end of Ocean Ave and followed the curve to the left. Straight ahead stood Misty Manor with a beautiful view of the lighthouse behind. The beacon light was turning, helping to guide boats in a dark daytime sky. Crime scene tape, which had been decorating the back yard for the last couple of weeks, had recently been removed from the property.

As Nick turned into the circular driveway located on the side of the Grand Victorian, he noticed an old Ford Explorer sitting in the driveway. He looked over at Megan. "Are you expecting any company?"

Megan sat straighter and stared at the car. "No, I have no idea who that belongs to. My father and his friend left in a limo last night. They weren't supposed to be back until Sunday, unless they rented a car and returned early, but honestly, I can't see my father stepping foot in that car. He is very particular, despite his lack of funds."

Nick snorted. "I can't wait to meet the guy. I haven't seen him since we were in high school."

Megan chuckled. "Believe me, I think you can wait. In the meantime, I'm glad you're with me. I have no idea who could be here."

"You think someone parked and crossed your property to the lighthouse?"

"Could be anyone, Nick. You'd be amazed at how many people stop and stare at Misty Manor and the North Point."

"The car is empty so someone got out. I'm wondering who and why."

"Yeah, well so am I," Megan said as Nick threw the car in park. Simultaneously, they unlocked their seat belts and stepped out of the Camaro.

"Let's leave the groceries in the car until we figure out what's going on," Nick said. He gently placed his hand on Megan's back as they turned the corner and heard an argument growing increasingly louder.

Chapter Nine

"There's no one here," a woman dressed in an expensive pantsuit said as Megan and Nick watched from the base of the porch steps.

"I don't believe this," an angry man yelled. "They said we'd be able to get rooms."

A second woman, wearing designer jeans and a gauzy top, dropped to the top step.

The first woman pulled away from the windows. "Call his cell. Maybe he'll answer if he sees it's you."

Nick let go of Megan and walked up to the steps. "Excuse me, can I help you folks?"

The man spun around. "Are you the manager here?"

Nick paused for a moment. "No, there is no manager here. This is a private residence and you are currently trespassing."

"What's your name?" The man demanded.

"It's Officer Nick Taylor of the Misty Point Police Department," Nick said as he crossed his arms. "Now, I'd like your name and some identification before I call the station."

The angry man hesitated a moment but then appeared to come to a decision. He reached into his back pocket as he started down the steps. "Kevin Shaw, from Austin, Texas," he said as he opened his wallet and pulled out his driver's license.

Nick spent a few moments scrutinizing the information and handed back the card. "Well, Mr. Shaw, why are you and your friends in New Jersey? Who are you looking for?" The two women watched from the porch.

"I'm here to meet up with my business partner," Kevin said.

"His name?" Nick asked.

"Randall Douglas, he's a real estate developer. He's looking at a potential deal here."

"I don't believe this," Megan said as she strode up to the group. "At Misty Manor?"

"I'm not sure," Kevin said. "He called and told us to get up here so we can check out the town. We flew up from Texas and tried to check into one of the hotels on the boardwalk, but there weren't any rooms available."

"It's August, at the Jersey Shore," Megan said as she raised her eyebrows. "You won't find any open hotel rooms."

"We quickly realized that so we called Randall and he told us to come here. His friend said we'd get rooms here. We thought it was a bed and breakfast."

Megan's face tightened as she clenched her jaw. "Dean, damn him."

Kevin turned toward her. "Yeah, Dean, that's his name. He told Randall the whole town was up for grabs."

Megan turned white as her stomach turned.

"So, will we be able to stay here or not?" Kevin asked as he looked at the women. "It's been a long day."

"Excuse me, I have to make a call," Megan said as she pulled out her cell phone and walked away. Nick watched her leave and shrugged in response to Kevin's question. Both men watched as Megan's call connected and she hissed into her phone. A few moments later, she ended the conversation, took a deep breath and walked back toward the house. She looked at Nick and said, "My father and Mr. Douglas are still in Atlantic City. They won't be back until tomorrow. They've asked me to accommodate Mr. Douglas's business associates for now."

Nick looked at Megan for a long moment. "It's up to you."

Megan spread her arms. "What am I supposed to do?"

"Whatever you want," Nick said. He nodded his head toward the guests indicating he could boot them all if she wanted him to.

Megan looked from Nick, to Kevin Shaw, and the two women on the front porch. They all looked tired. "Whatever," Megan said as she stepped around Kevin and walked up the front steps. She pulled out her keys and unlocked the front door.

"Thank you," the young woman jumped up. "I'm sorry, but I really need to use the bathroom."

Megan threw the front door wide. "C'mon in. Bring your bags, you can put them in the parlor for now."

The small group picked up their things and walked into Misty Manor. Megan waited for the women and said, "I'll show you to the powder room." As the women walked off, Kevin Shaw let out a low whistle as he looked around the foyer.

"This is some place," he said as he looked at Nick. "It would make a great executive getaway after some moderations."

"I wouldn't say that out loud," Nick said with a smile. "I don't think the place is for sale at the moment."

Kevin chuckled. "They all say that, but everyone's got their price. From what Randall's said, this guy Dean seems eager. He'll probably accept a low offer."

A small flare of anger surprised Nick as it flowed throughout his gut. He was glad Megan didn't hear Kevin's comment. He'd have to physically hold her back from assaulting him.

"Rose Stanford has only been gone three weeks." Nick tried to explain. "I don't think they've had time to make any decisions about the estate."

Kevin looked back at Nick. "That's interesting because this Dean is ready to sign on the dotted line. Douglas asked us to come up to give him an unbiased opinion but he made it seem as if he would lose the sale if he didn't decide in the next 48 hours."

"I'll admit I don't know details," Nick said as he eyed the man in front of him. "But I think Dean needs to discuss the situation with the family attorney first." Nick turned as he heard footsteps on the tile floor in the foyer.

Megan approached with the other two women in tow. "Well, we're back."

After a moment of silence, Megan turned to the strangers and extended her arms. "Hey, this is really awkward. Why don't we start over? My name is Megan Stanford. My grandmother, Rose Stanford, was the owner of Misty Manor and recently passed away three weeks ago. We were busy taking care of her as well as a few other family issues, so we haven't had time to freshen the place. We have plenty of rooms, but they're all dusty and stale. If you're willing to wait for a bit, I can call someone to come over and help get the rooms settled."

"Sounds good to me," Kevin said, turning to his companions. "What do you say?"

The young redhead shrugged, extended her hand to Megan and introduced herself. "Hi, I'm Savannah Williams. I'm Mr. Douglas's administrative assistant." She then turned and pointed to the other women. "This is Abigail Douglas, his wife."

The older woman, with bleached blonde hair piled in a nest on her head, nodded to Megan. "How do you do?"

"Thank you for having us, Miss Stanford," said Savannah. "It's been a long, exhausting trip from Texas and we'd be very grateful to stay here."

"Great," Megan said as she forced a smile. "Why don't you all head into the parlor and relax for a while. I need to make a few phone calls."

Abigail looked at Megan and said, "I don't mean to be a pain. Do you have anything we can munch on? I'm starving." She gave a sheepish smile. "We should have grabbed something in the airport."

Knowing she only had a can of tuna fish in the kitchen, Megan hesitated.

"I have plenty of groceries in the car," Nick said. "Let me go get the bags and we can fix something right away."

"Sounds fantastic," Abigail said and offered a smile.

"Thank you, Nick," Megan said, relieved they stopped at the grocery store. "In the meantime, I'll call Marie."

Chapter Ten

After asking Marie to run over and help, Megan called the attorney. "Teddy, I need some help," Megan whispered into her cell phone. She plopped down on the elegant duvet situated in the corner of the library.

"What's going on?" Teddy asked.

"Dean and Mr. Douglas left a couple hours after you did yesterday. They went to Atlantic City for steak and expensive cognac when they realized I had no food in the house."

"That's a good thing, right?"

"Yes, except I just found three people on my porch. They said they were told to come to New Jersey, by Mr. Douglas, to help him decide about purchasing Misty Manor."

"What?" Teddy asked. "Are you sure?"

"That's what they said. Mr. Douglas's business partner, his wife and his administrative assistant are here to help him conduct business."

"Even so, why are they at Misty Manor?"

"From what I'm told, the hotels were booked so Dean told them to come here."

"That's interesting," Teddy mused. "Are the hotels on the boardwalk really booked?"

Megan paused for a moment. "I have no idea. I didn't think to check, but they usually are crowded in August, especially on the weekends."

"I knew he was going to try something," Teddy said, disgust in his voice.

"Not a major surprise to anyone," Megan said. "But I have three extra people here and I have no cash. Marie agreed to come over and start cleaning a few of the rooms. Nick just donated a few bags of groceries, but my savings account is just about empty and I think Grandma Rose's checking account is frozen. I need some money for food."

"Who says you have to feed them? Let them order pizza or something. Better yet, send them down the boardwalk for a sausage sandwich."

Megan chuckled for a moment. "Not a bad idea, but honestly, I don't have enough money to buy a case of water or a pizza if I wanted."

"Okay, that's not a problem. Give me your bank account number and I'll transfer some money for you, but save it for yourself. Let them handle their own problems."

Megan let out a big sigh. She got up, grabbed her purse from the hall and rattled off some numbers. "Teddy, thank you so much."

"Technically, it's your money. Consider it an advance. When will your father be back?"

"According to him, they'll both be here tomorrow," Megan said.

"Don't tell him anything when he gets there." Teddy cautioned her.

"I wouldn't know what to tell him," Megan said, frustration evident in her voice. "Really, Teddy, what's going on?"

"Megan, we'll have a reading of the will later this week. In the meantime, no one has the authority to sell or change Misty Manor or any of Rose Stanford's holdings in any way."

"I believe you," Megan said. "But, I think you need to have a lengthy conversation with Dean."

Teddy chuckled. "That's okay, I'll let Rose tell him herself. I should go now. I just transferred some money to your account. I'll call you in a couple of days. Until then, avoid those people as much as possible."

Megan heard the click as she shouted, "Wait, Teddy." Her heart was pounding. *What did he mean let Rose tell him herself?*

Chapter Eleven

Megan walked into the parlor just as Nick delivered a tray with cheese, fruit and crackers to the coffee table. "That looks great, Nick. Thank you."

"You're very welcome," Nick said as he winked at Megan. He nodded his head toward the library. "How did things go?"

"Well enough, for now," Megan whispered. "Teddy transferred some money for me to live on, but I haven't checked how much yet." She watched as Savannah and Abigail made their way to the table and loaded paper plates with pieces of cheese and grapes.

Savannah looked up and shrugged an apology. "Sorry, but I'm starving."

Megan shook her head. "No problem. By all means, enjoy the food."

"Thanks, I appreciate it," Savannah said as she sniffed the air. "Something else smells great."

Megan looked at Nick who explained, "Marie arrived and is already whipping up dinner in the kitchen."

"Oh," Megan nodded and turned back to Savannah. "You're in for a treat. Marie's food tastes even better than it smells."

Savannah raised her eyebrows and nodded as she busily chewed several pieces of cheddar.

Abigail drifted toward the fireplace and now stood whispering with Kevin in vehement tones. Their conversation appeared to be politely heated as they held their plates. When she quietly responded, he frowned and shook his head.

Kevin suddenly turned his head as if he sensed someone was watching. Megan coughed and quickly dropped her eyes to the cheese platter sitting on the table. She grabbed a plate and placed a sampling of cheese and crackers on it. After a moment, Kevin elbowed Abigail and the two of them made their way over to the table. Just as Megan popped a grape in her mouth, Kevin spoke. "Can you tell us about Misty Manor?"

Trying not to choke at the abrupt question, Megan coughed into a napkin.

"I'm sorry," Abigail said. "What Kevin meant to say is thank you for dinner and letting us stay here. We're fascinated by your beautiful home and were wondering if you could tell us about some of its history."

Megan swallowed and looked at the pair expectantly watching her. She paused for a second before answering. "Sure, of course. My great grandfather, John Stanford, was a sea captain. He captained a trade charter which sailed back and forth to Europe. On one trip, he delivered special cargo as a favor to a wealthy industrialist in Philadelphia. As a gift, he was given a large parcel of land near the Atlantic Ocean in 1910. He developed the property into the town of Misty Point, NJ. When he married my great grandmother, Mary, he built this Grand Victorian home as a wedding gift for her. They named it Misty Manor. Together, they had a son named George, who married a woman named Rose. George and Rose were my grandparents. They named their son Dean, who happens to be my father.

Grandpa George disappeared a long time ago, but Grandma Rose stayed in Misty Point. She was a wonderful woman, a philanthropist and a much-loved benefactor to many before she passed.

"I'm so sorry to hear that, darlin'," Abigail said as she placed her hand on Megan's arm. "You sound as if you were very fond of each other."

"I loved Grandma Rose," Megan said as she began to tear up. "She'd been ill for a while." Megan looked around, reliving memories in her mind. "When I was a child, Misty Manor was full of life. Flowers on the porch, guests in the kitchen and one of the most beautiful views of the Atlantic you could find. Rose tried her best to keep things going, but her age and Hurricane Sandy put an end to that."

Abigail and Kevin nodded to empathize, then Kevin asked, "So what was Misty Manor like in the early nineteen-hundreds?"

Megan laughed nervously. "Well, I wasn't here at the time, but from what I understand it was one of the largest estates situated on the Jersey Shore. It boasted beautiful cultured gardens and a gorgeous lawn which sloped down to the beach and ocean below. John and Mary had a routine of drinks on the porch, followed by a gourmet meal in the formal dining room. Grandma Rose told me they would entertain often, sometimes hosting cribbage parties in the parlor."

"Cribbage?" Abigail questioned. "I thought that was an English game."

"Yes, that's true," Megan explained. "But Cribbage was very popular on American submarines. Its popularity spread to other sea captains and their wives in Britain and the United States. I believe it was created by the English poet and courtier, Sir John Suckling."

"Oh, my. Excuse me, dear, but what is a courtier?" Abigail asked with a smile as she placed her hand on her chest.

"Well, a courtier was usually a member of a royal court and acted as a companion to the king or queen." Megan explained.

"Well, *pardonne-moi,*" Abigail tittered in French laced with a southern accent.

Kevin inched forward and cleared his throat. "Ah, not to be indelicate, but was your grandmother still wealthy when she, ah, passed?"

Megan looked surprised. "Frankly, that's none of your business," she said, taking offense at his directness. "I have no idea what her worth was when she died and I wouldn't tell you if I did. However, I do know she owned Misty Manor as well as most Misty Point."

Kevin smirked as he took in her information. "Sorry, I didn't mean to be rude."

"Yes, I'm sure," Megan retorted as she turned and bounced into Nick who was standing right behind her.

"Sorry," Nick smiled. "Marie asked me to come find you. She has a few questions."

"Of course," Megan said as she silently thanked Nick for saving her from spending more time entertaining tactless strangers.

"Please, excuse us," Nick said as he placed his hand on the back of Megan's arm. "Enjoy the cheese and crackers. Marie will be sending in a cold pitcher of sweet tea."

Chapter Twelve

Megan fumed as she stood in the kitchen with Nick and Marie.

"Ignore him," Nick said. "We'll boot them out as soon as your father gets back with Mr. Douglas."

"They'd better all go back to Texas, pronto," Megan said with hands on hips.

Marie took a moment to dry her hands on a floral dish towel. "In the meantime, I was able to get four rooms prepared. At least, they'll stay in a clean room while they're here."

"Why four?" Megan asked. "There are only three of them."

"Yes, but I wanted to have an extra room," Marie said, nodding her head toward Nick. "It might be nice to have someone here watching over us."

Megan's face reddened as she realized what Marie was getting at.

"Sounds good to me," Nick smiled broadly. "My own room in Misty Manor."

"Don't get too excited," Megan said as she smiled.

"I'll stay in the room I used when I was taking care of Rose, poor dear," Marie said as she clucked and shook her head. "And tomorrow, I'll clear another two rooms, one for your father and the other as a spare."

"It's starting to sound like a circus," Megan said as she frowned. "We're not running a hotel."

"Your father is responsible for all this," Nick said. "He should be doing the cleaning."

"Tell me about it," Megan whispered as she looked at Marie. "I hope you're not making another fabulous meal. We want these people to leave. Don't encourage them to stay any longer."

Marie raised her eyebrows. "You don't know the half of it, honey. They came in here earlier asking for drinks."

"You made them a pitcher of sweet tea," Megan said. "What else do they want?"

Marie laughed. "Well, Mrs. Douglas offered me fifty bucks for a vodka gimlet, Mr. Shaw wanted bourbon, and sweet Savannah asked about mojitos."

"You have to be kidding me," Megan sputtered. "So, what did you tell them?"

"I explained the best I could do today was a bottle of wine with a screwcap."

Nick chuckled behind them.

"I told them where to find the liquor store, but they didn't take the bait, so no drinks for them."

"You didn't tell them the liquor store delivers?" Nick asked.

"Of course not," Marie said. "If they want a drink that bad, they can let their fingers and credit card do the walking. They have that banged up truck in the driveway as well."

"You're the best," Megan said as she gave her a big hug.

"And I don't think you should stay here playing hostess either. You're already being way too polite. Why don't you and Nick go out tonight? I'll feed them a meal and get them to their rooms. They look pretty tired to me anyway."

Megan glanced at Nick. "I don't know."

"I think it's a great idea," Nick said. "Georgie, Amber and Tommy have been trying to get you out for weeks now. Let's go out for drinks."

"Do you think you'd be okay if you were alone with them here?"

Marie chuckled. "I think you have to worry more about them being alone with me. I'll be watching them to make sure they're not creeping around the house. I don't trust them."

Megan turned around just as Nick clicked off his phone. "The decision's made. We're meeting everyone at The Clamshell in an hour. Tommy can't be there because the band has a gig."

"Excellent, now you two get out of the kitchen and let me finish my work here," Marie said as she ushered them through the door.

Chapter Thirteen

"Hey, it's so great to see you," Georgie said as she bear hugged Megan on the sidewalk outside of the bar.

Megan smiled. "Thanks, Georgie. It's great to see you, too. I'm sorry I haven't met up with you, but it's been difficult."

"I get it," Georgie said, nodding her head. "We all feel terrible and loved Grandma Rose. I can only imagine how you've been feeling."

Nick stood behind Megan and gently placed his hand on the small of her back to show support. The three of them turned as they heard a female voice yell out to them. Amber, wearing a designer V-neck cold shoulder blouse, was running toward them with a big smile on her face. "Ahh, I can't believe it. Megan, you're here!"

The group couldn't help but laugh at their friend's enthusiasm. "Yes, Amber, I'm here."

Amber ran right at Megan and grabbed her around the middle. "I missed you so much. Georgie picks on me when you're not around."

Megan laughed as she pried her friend's arms off. "I'm sure you can take care of yourself." She stepped back and eyed Amber's outfit. "Very nice and chic." Megan made a show of looking around. "Where's Tommy? I can't believe he's not here."

"He would be, if he could be," Amber rushed to explain. "You'll never believe this, but Tommy and the Tides are playing at the Arena tonight. They're opening for a really famous band."

"I thought Tommy and the Tides were a really famous band," Megan said.

"They will be," Amber laughed. "One day, they'll be the main event."

"And how about you and Tommy? Are you the main event yet?"

"Are you kidding me? He's just at the point where he won't run if we're alone together."

"Oh boy," Megan laughed as Nick broke into their conversation.

"There's a large group coming up behind us. Let's go in and get a table."

"Sounds good to me," Georgie said. She reached out and pulled on the gold-plated handle attached to the wooden door, which led to the bar. They squeezed past the counter and paraded into the dining room, a hostess immediately greeting them. After asking for the number in their party, she escorted them to a nearby table which was centered under a dim blue scone. As the foursome squeezed into the booth, the hostess placed menus on the table and informed them a waitress would be over to take their drink order. The special of the night was Red Snapper with a Garlic Aioli.

"Whatever they're cooking smells great," Georgie said as she opened a menu.

"That's easy for you to say, you can eat without gaining weight," Amber pouted.

Georgie frowned at her friend. "I think the ten-mile run I took this afternoon has more to do with controlling my weight."

"Hey, I go to the gym," Amber protested.

"Yea, the corporate gym." Georgie laughed. "Last time I went, you stretched farther to check your butt in the mirror than you did in that Zumba class."

Megan and Nick laughed as their waitress approached the table. After a few minutes, they placed their orders and surrendered their menus.

Georgie turned toward Megan and gently prodded. "So, how are you doing?"

Megan shrugged as she looked at one of her best friends from high school. "What can I say? I have some good days and some bad days. The past couple of months have brought back so many memories."

"For all of us," Georgie said. "I miss the days when we used to hang out on the beach after school."

"We had great tans back then," Amber piped in with a laugh.

"And great bonfires at night," Georgie said as she looked at Megan. "We were lucky you owned a private beach."

"That was after we went to the boardwalk, ate sausage sandwiches and went on all the rides," Nick said with a laugh. "We did have a blast."

Megan nodded slowly. "Yes, we did." Megan lapsed into silence as she processed her thoughts.

The waitress appeared at their side with drinks and placed them on the table. She artfully arranged small rectangular plates around three larger platters of appetizers the group had agreed to share. They spent the next several minutes doling out tasty bites of mushrooms stuffed with crabmeat, cold shrimp and zesty onion rings.

"So, what's going on?" Amber asked as she daintily ate a shrimp and looked at Megan.

"What do you mean?" Megan asked.

"There have been lights on in your house and cars in and out," Amber said.

"Are you stalking me?" Megan laughed as she reached for an onion ring.

"No, that's actually the word on the street," Amber said.

"What do you mean?"

Amber glanced nervously at Georgie. "Why don't you tell her?"

Georgie frowned at her friend. "Thanks, I appreciate it." She turned toward Megan and cleared her throat. "Okay, so there are a lot of people talking in town. They saw your father walking around with some guy from Texas. They went up and down the boardwalk and were checking out the hotels."

Megan shook her head in disbelief. "When? They've been in Atlantic City all weekend."

"I guess they took a tour of Misty Point before they left," Georgie said as she shrugged her shoulders. "Apparently, they went into the Royal Island Hotel and made some comments about how they would knock it down and start over. The staff got upset and the hotel manager threw them out."

"I think they called the police station as well," Nick said as he cupped his beer. "Everyone has been on pins and needles since Rose died, wondering what's going to happen to the town."

"What makes everyone think Mr. Douglas will be able to buy it?" Megan asked as her cheeks flamed.

"Your father has not been discreet about his intentions," Nick said. "And as far as most people are concerned, you've disappeared since you sequestered yourself."

"Wow, that makes sense," Megan said shaking her head. "And the sad part is I have no idea what's going on. Teddy hasn't read the will, yet."

"Your father must be anticipating good news if he's showing off the town," Amber said as she sipped her drink.

"Not to mention the three strangers staying at Misty Manor," Megan said.

"Three strangers? What's that all about?" Amber leaned forward.

"Nick and I went out this morning and when we got back, there were three strangers on my porch. They said there was no room at the hotels so they were told to stay at Misty Manor."

"Who are these people?" Georgie asked.

"The guy with my father is Randall Douglas. He asked his wife, his business partner and his assistant to join him in Misty Point, because my father wants to sell him Misty Manor as well as some of the land in town. They've been at the house all day, requesting food and drink like we're running a bed and breakfast."

"Hey, opening Misty Manor as a bed and breakfast would be a great idea," Amber said.

"Amber, I thought you were on my side," Megan said.

"I am. I didn't mean for them to do it, I meant for you."

"What?" Megan said. "I can't make plans for the house. I'm not sure where I'll be living next month."

"Maybe you should call that lawyer of yours and get some sort of a preview," Georgie said. "Then you can throw that motley crew out."

Megan sipped her drink. "I talked to him earlier, but he didn't say anything too telling. Maybe I can call him again tomorrow."

"I suggest you do whatever you can and do it fast," Georgie said as she reached for another shrimp.

Chapter Fourteen

Megan rolled over when she heard a noise in the hall. Sunday morning, and all she wanted to do was stay in bed and sleep late. She had fun the night before at The Clamshell and had relaxed enough to drop into a deep sleep when she and Nick arrived back to Misty Manor. In addition to the few drinks, Megan enjoyed having Nick nearby. His presence made her more at ease, a peace she had not known for quite some time.

After a moment, she inclined her head and strained to listen. Why would there be noise in the hall? Marie said all the guests were staying on the second floor of Misty Manor.

Megan was in her childhood bedroom on the third floor of the Grand Victorian mansion. There was a total of four bedrooms on the third floor and one tiled bathroom with a claw foot tub and shower. The only room on the floor above was the attic and you had to walk through that area to reach the cupola. From there the view of the ocean was breathtaking, a final set of twisted stairs would guide you to the roof, and out onto the widow's walk.

Megan heard another creak, the sound clearly from the hallway. She jumped up and threw a sweatshirt over her thin t-shirt and walked to the door. She placed her ear against the door and then turned the knob slowly to peek into the hall. At first, she didn't see anyone. Megan stepped into the hallway and turned in time to see a shadow fall over the threshold of the room next to hers so she waited a heartbeat and then tip-toed on the carpet to the door.

Inside the room, Abigail Douglas was pulling out each drawer of the dresser and rifling through the contents. She would push the drawer back in and proceed to the next. The woman paused at the window long enough to take in the scenery. The rain had stopped for now and she seemed to enjoy the view of the lawn, sloping down to a gorgeous beach made of fine sand and ending in curls of blue-green surf.

When she moved to the bedside table and bent to open the drawer, Megan finally spoke. "Can I help you find something?"

Abigail jumped up, twirled around and placed her hand over her heart. "Oh, darlin', you scared me to death." She fanned her face as she pointed to the window and said, "I got to being curious and wanted to see the view from a higher floor. It's quite beautiful out there."

"Yes, it is," Megan agreed. "It sounded as if you were opening drawers and searching for something."

Abigail waved her hand at Megan. "Oh, that's just silly. When I walked in the room I noticed one of the drawers wasn't closed and I didn't want anyone to hurt themselves so I pushed it in."

Megan held her tongue and decided not to tell her she was watching for several minutes. "Thank you for that, but I think it would be best if you joined the rest of the guests downstairs. Marie most likely has coffee and breakfast on the sideboard in the dining room." She stepped back and ushered Abigail into the hall. Megan followed her and firmly pulled the bedroom door closed behind them.

"This is a beautiful home, so much history and treasures to be explored," Abigail said as she scanned the hall. "Oh, what's behind the door at the top of the stairs?"

Megan shrugged. "Just an attic. A lot of dusty, dirty things. Hasn't been cleaned in years. I'm sure there's nothing of interest." Megan continued to herd Abigail toward the main stairs. "My room is on this floor and most of these rooms are kept closed so you don't need to come back up here."

"Oh, I'd be happy to help you clean out the attic," Abigail whined as Megan guided her to the top of the stairs.

I'll bet, Megan thought as she smiled outwardly. "Thank you, but until the estate is settled, none of us can touch anything in the house. You understand, I'm sure." Megan continued to smile as she watched Abigail descend the stairs. Once she turned the corner and continued down to the main floor, Megan rushed back down the hall. Before going into her bedroom, she went to the attic door and checked the new lock which had been installed before Megan returned home. Without the key, it held fast and Megan hoped it continued to do so. The nerve of these people. Marie had been right not to trust them and thank goodness, Teddy warned her to lock Grandma Rose's room.

Megan grabbed some towels and headed for the bathroom. As much as she wanted to get downstairs to keep an eye on these guests, she needed a hot shower to face the day.

Chapter Fifteen

Dressed in her favorite jeans and t-shirt, Megan descended the stairs to the second-floor landing. She went to Grandma Rose's room and checked to make sure the door was still locked. As Megan turned away from the door she felt a pair of muscular arms surround her and pull her close to a tight male chest. Her heart skipped a beat until she felt a warm breath in her hair. "Your hair smells great." Nick said as he nuzzled Megan's neck. "I could get used to this arrangement."

Megan pulled back a bit. "Nick, you won't believe what just happened."

"Wait a second," Nick said as he looked at her and smiled. Before she could speak again, he laced his fingers in her hair, gently pulled her close and tasted her warm lips. When he pulled back, he was still smiling as he said, "Good morning, did you sleep well?"

Megan's stomach clutched as her face flamed. "Ah...ah,"

"Speechless, huh?"

Megan laughed as she lightly punched him in the shoulder. "I wouldn't flatter yourself too much. It was more unexpected." At that moment, Megan thought she suddenly understood why women used to swoon, but she'd never let him know that.

Laughing, Nick gave her a nice body hug. "Really, I could get use to waking up to this." When Megan squinted at him, he said, "Okay, so what happened?"

"I was sound asleep and I heard someone creeping outside my door."

"Who was it? I'll kill him," Nick said as he tucked a piece of her hair behind her ear.

Megan felt her face getting warm again. "It wasn't a guy. It was Abigail Douglas and she was tossing one of the bedrooms upstairs."

"Really, why?"

"I don't know." Megan shrugged. "There's nothing personal in those rooms, but they don't know that. I got the feeling she thinks there are valuable items and wanted to help herself. I confronted her and she lied to me. I escorted her to the stairs and told her not to come back. Her hands were empty so I'm pretty sure she didn't find anything."

Nick shook his head. "The second any one of these people put their hands on something that doesn't belong to them, I can arrest them."

"I appreciate the offer, Nick. I don't understand why people think they can help themselves to other people's property."

"It's more common than you think."

"As you well know, Fran Stiles had her sticky fingers in Grandma Rose's possessions when I first got here. Grandma Rose knew it too, but she said she had hidden all the good stuff. I have no idea what Fran may have taken except for what you found in her apartment."

"Some people don't operate on a moral compass," Nick said as he gently held Megan by the upper arms.

"Let's go downstairs and keep a watch on these people," Megan said as she stared into his beautiful eyes.

"I'd rather watch you," Nick said. "But I can't stay. I didn't have time to let you know, but one of the guys called out sick so I have to work today."

"But you don't have your uniform," Megan said.

"I know. That's one of the reasons I looked for you this morning," Nick said, looking down at her. "I have to grab my stuff and head to the station. Looks like it's going to be a twelve-hour shift, so I can't be here today." He leaned forward and gave her a kiss on the forehead. "But I'll be in touch as soon as my shift is over."

Megan was disappointed but nodded and grinned. "I wouldn't want you under my feet all day anyway. Go to work."

"Hmmnn," Nick mused. He wrapped his arm around her shoulders as they made their way to the grand staircase. "Trying to get me out of here?"

"Why yes, I have many suitors coming to visit today," Megan teased. "Your presence would put a damper on their visits."

Chapter Sixteen

Sunday morning passed quickly. Megan spent time in the kitchen with Marie, washing dishes and talking quietly about their guests. Megan told Marie of Abigail's wandering and the two made plans to keep an extra close eye on the house, especially now that Dean and Randall were due to return.

After breakfast, Savannah changed into shorts and a bathing suit top and left the house to walk on the beach. Abigail spent time on the front porch watching the ocean and then walking the length of the house while examining everything in her reach. Kevin spent most of the morning on his cell phone, checking e-mail, tapping various apps, and frowning while repeatedly looking at his watch.

In the early afternoon, Abigail opened the front door and yelled out, "Megan, are you here?" She then walked into the foyer and was followed by a man as she continued to call out. "Megan, where are you? Someone is here to see you."

Megan dried her hands on a dishtowel and looked at Marie with eyebrows raised. The two had prepared a tray of sandwiches and fruit to feed their unwanted guests for lunch. Better to provide something simple than have them pawing through the kitchen.

Wondering who Abigail brought into the house, Megan quickly ran out to the foyer. The last thing she needed was another acquaintance of Randall Douglas dropping in but nothing prepared her for the shock of seeing the mayor of Misty Point, Andrew Davenport, standing in her foyer.

The man was arrogant and self-assuming and it was a fact there was bad blood between their families which immediately made Megan's heart rate spike.

Megan approached the two in the foyer, looked Mr. Davenport straight in the eye and said, "Why are you in this house?"

"How are you, Megan?" The mayor nodded curtly and looked around the room. "Nice place. I haven't been inside Misty Manor since I was young."

"The way it should be and in case you aren't sure, you're not welcome here now," Megan said as she looked toward Abigail. "Why did you bring Mr. Davenport in my house?"

Abigail looked at Megan and shrugged. "How do I know who's allowed in your house? The man walked up to the porch and asked if you were home. I thought I was helping out."

Megan considered her comment while walking her to the front door. "Thank you. Please go back outside and enjoy the ocean. I'll take care of this." Megan opened the door and waited for Abigail to leave but Megan could tell she wanted to eavesdrop by the way she looked back toward the foyer while dragging her feet.

After closing the door, Megan marched over to Andrew Davenport. "Why are you here?"

Andrew frowned and then said, "Is it true? I had to come myself to find out if it was true."

"Is what true?" Megan asked while shaking her head.

"Don't act so innocent." Andrew Davenport turned red as he began to shout. "It's all over town. You're going to sell Misty Manor and redevelop the property." He jabbed his index finger in her direction. "Your father may have inherited this property and half of the town, but don't think for a minute you'll be able to start knocking down buildings and putting up whatever you please. We have laws. There are protected areas and I'll personally hold you up in court for years to come if I have to."

Megan put her hand up to silence him. "First, I don't need to provide an explanation to you or anyone else in this town. Secondly, I have no idea what you're going on about. There are absolutely no arrangements being made involving the sale of Misty Manor or Misty Point." Feeling herself get aggravated, Megan raised her voice. "How dare you come to my home and threaten me!"

"Don't try to deny it. Half the townspeople saw your father touring Randall Douglas all over the place."

"So, what? That doesn't mean anything. My father said he was a friend."

Andrew let out a laugh, loud enough to indicate his outrage and disbelief. "Just a friend? Do you know who Randall Douglas is?"

Megan shook her head as she answered. "Honestly, I don't. He popped in here for an hour on Friday, with my father, and as far as I know they're still in Atlantic City."

"Well, let me enlighten you. He happens to be one of the biggest commercial real estate developers of all time. Did you get that? Commercial. He has a reputation for ruining some of the most beautiful parts of the country with his gaudy hotels and ugly developments. He buys property, builds cookie cutter houses and then flips them for millions of dollars."

"I don't know what you're talking about. Misty Manor is not for sale. It physically can't be, our attorney hasn't read the will yet."

Andrew took a deep breath. "So, there's a chance?"

Megan shook her head. "Chance of what?"

"Of listening to other proposals," Andrew said. "The town council has some ideas about redeveloping some of the town."

"Really?" Megan asked in disbelief.

"And if an opportunity presented itself, I was considering making a personal bid as well," Andrew said, his voice more controlled.

"I'm sure you wouldn't be considering anything unless it made you a ton of money," Megan said sarcastically. "It doesn't matter, because nothing is for sale, Mr. Davenport." Megan turned and made her way to the door. "Thanks for stopping in, but please don't ever come back."

Andrew clenched his jaw and made his way toward the front door. "Fine, but I mean what I said. You'll regret the day you try to pull a fast one over the people in this town."

"Oh really? Try something and you'll wind up in jail, next to your son. Good day, Mr. Davenport." Megan yanked on the front door which almost sent Abigail Douglas tumbling inside the foyer. Abigail righted herself, dusted off her slacks and pretended she had tripped just outside the door. Megan waited until they both left the foyer and were on the porch before she slammed the door closed. As she turned to walk back to the kitchen, she couldn't help but notice Abigail hanging over Andrew Davenport on his way to the street.

Chapter Seventeen

Megan kept busy in the kitchen as she fumed over Davenport's visit. She was thrilled there was a sink full of dishes to redirect her energy, otherwise she would have punched something. Marie told her she would do them but they needed a few extra ingredients for dinner. Megan jumped at the opportunity to give Marie some cash and hurry her out the back door so she could work off her anger. Megan still wanted to punch something, but thankfully, she had enough will power to restrain from clocking Andrew Davenport. While rinsing a dish, a sudden clamor erupted from the foyer. Megan held back a soft curse, threw the sponge into the sink and grabbed a dishtowel to dry her hands. She walked into the foyer, wishing this eternal weekend would come to a swift end. She quickly found the source of the noise when she spotted her father and Randall Douglas near the front door. They were laughing and slapping each other on the back. They must have had a great trip to Atlantic City.

Megan stood in the middle of the foyer, crossed her arms and cleared her throat. Her father, Dean, looked up and noticed her standing there. "Megan, how are you? We're back and we bought you a gift." He walked over and handed her a one pound box of salt water taffy.

"Wow, a pound of taffy. Oh, how thoughtful," Megan said as she looked over the box. She made a face when she read the side panel. *Courtesy of your hotel.*

"You got me, sweetheart," Dean said as he and Randall broke out in ripples of laughter.

As the trio stood in the foyer, the rest of the guests wandered inside. Savannah walked through the front door. Wearing a very small bikini, no cover up, sunglasses pushed back on her head, she placed a bag holding a few magazines on the marble foyer table. A sunburn glared from her shoulders and set off her red hair.

Abigail Douglas appeared next. She approached her husband wearing the epitome of sarcasm and plastic smiles. "So good to see you, dear." She leaned forward and offered her cheek to her husband and waited for his hearty kiss.

"Gabby, how are you? Honey, you're a sight for sore eyes." Randall said as he tugged at his belt buckle with one hand and slapped his thigh with the other.

Abigail walked over to Savannah and eyed her from head to toe. "Speaking of sore eyes, you look cold, sweetie. Maybe you should put some clothes on." Abigail tossed her head, turned on her heel and walked back to her husband as Savannah shot a dirty look at the back of her head. "Did you have a good trip, dear?"

Randall nearly guffawed. "Sure did, I think we're going to enjoy spending time in New Jersey. I'm happy you all got here so quickly."

"You called and we came a' running," Savannah said posing by the table.

Just then, Kevin stormed out of the parlor. "Damn it, where've you been Randall? I've had three clients busting my chops while I've been waiting for you to get back here."

Randall threw up a hand and waved him off. "Let 'em wait."

"Let them wait? We're talking millions of dollars." Kevin glowered as he looked at Randall. "Listen, we've got to take ten minutes to talk shop. We have some calls to make and decisions to be made. You can get back to the ladies in a bit." Kevin placed his hand on the back of Randall's elbow and steered him into the parlor.

"Well, I'm going to take a long, hot shower," Savannah said as she picked up her bag and started up the grand staircase.

"Cheap, little tart," Abigail said as she watched Savannah climb the stairs.

"What did you say?" Savannah said as she whirled around and faced Abigail.

"Nothing much, sweetie," Abigail said as she waved her on. "Better go wash up and get some decent clothes on. No one here is impressed with your wares."

Megan silently agreed but couldn't help noticing her father was almost panting as he ogled Savannah's body on the staircase. Attempting to break his sordid concentration, Megan called out to him. "Hey Dad, do you mind if we have a few private words in the library?"

Dean looked at her but didn't appear to understand at first. Megan raised her voice a bit. "Please, Dad, over here."

Dean flashed a final smile at Savannah and with a small wave, turned and walked toward Megan with a frown. "What can you possibly want?"

"What the hell is going on around here?" Megan asked, fury in her hushed voice. "First, you drag your friend all over the place and then his three cohorts show up unannounced at the door."

Dean scowled at his daughter. "Look, I've got something big going on and I don't want you screwing it up. If you're lucky, I may throw a little something your way. Either shut up, smile, and make these people feel very welcomed or do me a favor, pack your bag and get out for a while."

"So, you're trying to sell Misty Manor and the other land Grandma owned?" Megan asked.

"The sooner I get rid of Misty Manor, the better," Dean said with disgust. "I hated growing up in this house and I can't wait to get out."

Randall emerged from the parlor. Kevin then appeared, looking furious, but already punching numbers into his phone. As he started to speak to someone, he slipped out onto the front porch for some privacy.

Randall began to climb the grand staircase but stopped when he heard Megan and Dean speaking under the stairs.

"Well, in case you were interested you had another visitor today," Megan said crossing her arms.

"Are you going to tell me who it was or just stand there striking a pose?"

Megan blew out a breath to calm the pain gathering in her chest. "It was Andrew Davenport."

"And what did that ass want?"

"He was raving mad at you. He said people are saying you're planning on selling Misty Manor. First, he threatened to sue and block you in court, but then he made sure to let me know he wanted in on the action. Can you believe the nerve of that man?"

"Nothing the Davenports do surprise me," Dean said. "But I've got a sweet deal already lined up."

"How can you have a deal lined up when Teddy hasn't read the will?" Megan asked as she shook her head. "I just signed the papers Friday."

"What papers?" Dean asked. "What are you talking about?"

"Remember the rain storm? The one you barged in on? Teddy was here to have me sign papers and he left to have them filed immediately."

Randall began to frown on the stairs.

"What papers did you sign?" Dean demanded.

"I didn't read them all," Megan said. "I trust Teddy. Grandma Rose always did."

"It's hard for me to believe I would've raised a fool," Dean shouted. He turned as he heard a noise behind him. Both Dean and Megan watched Randall step off the stairs and turn the corner toward them.

"Didn't mean to eavesdrop Dean, but I thought you had everything wrapped up in terms of the property."

"Well, I almost do," Dean said. He tried to laugh and clap Randall on the back, but suddenly his friend didn't seem to be buying the routine.

"And now I hear there's competition. Is this a cheap attempt to raise the price again?"

Dean tried to calm his friend down. "No, Randall. I assure you this is simply a rough patch in the road. I have to call our family attorney and straighten a few things out, but everything's fine." Dean threw his arm around Randall's shoulders. "Let's go into the parlor and relax. I'm sure we'll have something to eat soon and we can get back to business later."

As the two men walked off, Megan heard Randall say, "I sure as hell hope you aren't wasting my time here."

Dean answered with a nervous laugh as he turned around and shot Megan a dirty look.

Chapter Eighteen

Megan went back to the kitchen and waited for Marie to return from grocery shopping. When she knocked on the back door, Megan helped to carry the paper bags and together, they placed them on the counter and began to empty their contents. Megan took the tray of sandwiches they had made earlier and placed it on the sideboard in the dining room. She heard someone knocking on the front door while making her way back to the kitchen. Changing course, she headed toward the front, wondering who the next guest could possibly be, when she almost collided with Abigail Douglas who ran towards the front door.

"I'll get that," she said. "You needn't bother yourself."

"Excuse me?" Megan asked as Abigail adopted an in-charge attitude.

Abigail realized her mistake. "I'm sorry, but I placed an order for everyone to enjoy so I thought I would get the door and take care of it."

Megan raised her eyebrows and extended her hand toward the door, indicating Abigail could take the lead. Abigail opened the front door and found a delivery person on the porch with a large cardboard box and three bags of ice. Abigail spoke with him for a few minutes when he presented the bill. She pulled out a wad of cash and paid his fee with a generous tip which motivated him to bring the box indoors and place it on the foyer table. He then went outside and picked up the three bags of ice and plopped them on the marble floor next to the front door.

Megan quickly spoke out. "Hey, please take that right to the kitchen. I'll be happy to show you where it is." She then led the young man down the hall. "Please put the ice in the sink." Once the ice was placed, he left through the back door. When Abigail entered the kitchen several minutes later, Megan had emptied the ice from one of the bags into a serving bowl and added tongs.

When Abigail saw the bowl, and smiled, Megan asked, "Whatever are you serving?"

"Whatever you want."

Megan followed her into the dining room and found a bevy of liquor bottles set up on the side bar. Abigail added the ice and then asked Megan where she could find glasses. "Everyone is so uptight. I thought this would be a good ice breaker." Abigail laughed at her own joke. "Seriously, this crew needs a few drinks to calm them down."

"You'll find some glasses in there," Megan said, pointing to a china cabinet on the side of the room. "We've used mugs and plastic cups since I moved back to New Jersey. I haven't had time to go through the cabinets and I'm not sure anyone has for a long time."

Abigail rummaged through the shelves and found several rocks glasses for whiskey, long-stemmed wine glasses, shot glasses, a brandy snifter, a few chipped martini glasses and a pair of highball glasses. "Is it okay if I pull some of these out?"

"I guess so," Megan said. "We'll bring them into the kitchen to wash them. Marie may know if there are more glasses inside."

"I'll bet there's a whole stash of glasses and other neat stuff in this house from years gone by," Abigail said as she pulled several things from the cabinet.

"I've been told there were grand parties at Misty Manor many years ago. I'm sure there may be a few things left from that time," Megan said as she looked at the contents of the cabinet. She imagined parties where the men retreated to the parlor with cognac while the women stayed behind in the dining room to talk. It was likely her great grandfather brought liquor and glasses back from Europe on his voyages.

Megan noticed Abigail's eyes light up with interest. After Abigail's adventure in the upstairs bedroom, Megan wanted to believe she had a strong interest in history but was concerned it may be more a case of sticky fingers. Now she would have to watch her more closely.

The two women carried the glasses through the hall and into the kitchen. Megan placed the other two bags of ice in the freezer so they had ample room to wash the glasses in the sink. Marie came bustling around the corner to check on a roast in the oven and asked what was happening. Megan explained about the liquor delivery.

"Oh, then I'll take care of this in a jiffy," Marie said as she began to fill the sink with hot water. "Why don't the two of you go to the parlor and I'll let you know when everything is ready?" Marie looked at Megan and nodded her head to send a message to escort Abigail into the parlor.

Megan nodded back in silence and after picking up the ice bucket and one clean glass, she drew Abigail away from the kitchen. The two walked over to the dining room and Megan was careful to place the ice bucket on an area away from the highly-polished wood. She pulled a thick tablecloth from a drawer, covered the sideboard and rearranged the liquor bottles so there would be no chance of spillage. Megan placed the delivery box on the side as there was an assortment of drink related products inside.

"Before we go back into the parlor, I'd like to make myself a drink," Abigail said eyeing the assortment of bottles she ordered from the local store.

"You're of legal age, I can't stop you," Megan said as she shrugged her shoulders.

"You know, it wouldn't hurt you any if you decided to have a small drink for yourself," Abigail suggested as she dug into the box and whipped out a cocktail shaker. She filled it with ice, a generous amount of vodka, and a small amount of simple syrup. She picked up a lime and took a knife from the sideboard. After slicing the lime, she added it to the shaker, closed the top and shook it rapidly up and down. She took the clean rocks glass, filled it with ice and strained the drink from the shaker into the glass. Abigail tipped the glass in Megan's direction and took a large gulp of the liquor. "Oh my, that is good," Abigail said as she picked up the shaker and strained the rest of the liquor into her glass. Turning to Megan, she asked, "Do you want me to make you one?"

Megan shook her head, eyes wide. "No, thank you. I haven't had enough to eat today and I don't know what time dinner will be ready. Can I get you something to eat?"

Abigail lifted her drink and took another long swallow. "Don't worry about me. I can handle my liquor."

"Okay, why don't we go into the parlor and wait for Marie to call us?" Megan suggested as she began to escort Abigail away from the sideboard before she started another shaker.

The two crossed the hall and entered the parlor to find Dean, Randall, Kevin and Savannah already present. Savannah immediately noticed Abigail's drink. "Where did you get that?"

Abigail's laugh was predatory as she said, "There's a whole bar set up in the dining room." Tipping the glass toward the other guests, she said, "bottoms up," and walked toward the corner of the room.

"I think I'll go make myself a little something," Savannah said as she rose from the couch. "Kevin, do you want me to get something for you?"

"No, I'm fine." Kevin waved her away as he turned toward the window.

Dean immediately got up and followed her. He turned to Randall as he left saying, "I'll bring back a tummy warmer for you."

Randall hitched his belt buckle up. "Sounds good to me."

Chapter Nineteen

"Hey, can you pass those potatoes?" Dean said, pointing to Kevin who sat on the opposite side of the table.

"Sure, you may want to try the salad too," Kevin mumbled under his breath.

"At least, he's adding food to his liquid dinner," Abigail said as she chuckled at her own joke.

Megan pushed her chair back from the dining room table and silently fumed. Her father, Dean, and his friend Randall hadn't stopped drinking since Abigail announced the presence of the instant *bar* in the dining room. Savannah had been generous with herself as well. Megan was surprised when she realized Abigail had no problem restraining herself after the first drink, but continued to spur everyone else on, pretending to need her drink and profess how much she enjoyed being able to vacation at the Jersey Shore. *What was she up to?*

Megan and Marie went about serving dinner, collecting plates, and retrieving more ice. Noticing the liquor was beginning to take hold, Megan put on a pot of coffee while Marie whipped up dessert to help balance the meal.

As Marie gently set a tray of decadent brownies on the table, Dean leaned back, patted his bloated abdomen and yelled out. "Marie, you always were a fantastic cook and nothing has changed." Megan almost dropped the coffee pot she was holding when she saw her father leer at Marie as if they were back in school. More shocking was when Marie nervously smiled back as if she was flattered by the attention.

"Marie, what kind of digestives do you have for us?" Dean winked at her as she passed and would have slapped her butt had it not been for the dirty look Megan shot her father. He caught her look and stopped, hand suspended in mid-air as Marie leaned toward the table to remove the remaining plates set in front of him.

Marie stood up with plates gathered in her arms, a bit confused. "I don't think we have anything here. I didn't know there was any liquor in the house."

"Oh, no need to fret." Abigail laughed as she stood, rummaged around her table of liquors and pulled a fine bottle of sherry from the back. She turned back, handed the bottle to Megan. "Can you open this for us, dear?" Returning to her seat, she said, "We'll need some fresh glasses, too."

Megan clenched her jaw as she was waved away by Abigail who acted as if she were the Grande dame and owner of Misty Manor. She turned and made her way to the kitchen to stop herself from hurling the bottle back towards Abigail.

"Can you believe the nerve of that woman?" Megan placed the bottle on the counter and turned around to face Marie. "Who the hell does she think she is?"

"I don't know, but she does want to be in charge, doesn't she?" Marie placed the last of the remaining dishes in the sink and filled it with hot sudsy water. "I don't know what's going to happen to Misty Manor, but I hope someone puts a dishwasher in here, someday."

"And what was with that look from my father?" Megan demanded as she crossed her arms.

Marie blushed as she shrugged. "He's a little drunk, but he was always like that."

"C'mon, don't let him do that to you. He looks at women like he's at a beef auction."

"I know," Marie said quietly. "I'm sorry."

"Don't be sorry, be proud and don't let him degrade you like that." Megan seethed as she paced around the kitchen table. "I have to call Teddy tomorrow. Monday morning, he should be back in town. There has to be a way we can get these people out of here."

Marie turned back to the sink. "Let's hope so. They're not a nice group of people."

Their conversation was interrupted as Abigail floated into the kitchen. "Megan, do you have that bottle of sherry opened yet? We've been waiting an awful long time."

Megan turned to Abigail. "I'm sorry, I can't seem to find any sherry glasses."

"Oh, that's okay. We can use a tulip wine glass," Abigail said as she made her way to a cabinet filled with glasses. She pulled out five glasses and gave them to Marie to wash and dry. "I assume you won't be drinking sherry. It seems a bit too stodgy for you."

Megan's mouth twitched but nothing came out before Abigail interrupted. "Thankfully, this is a sweet sherry so serving at room temperature will be fine." Abigail turned back toward Megan. "I know you're young, but you may want to take some courses in entertaining so you are familiar with how to be the proper hostess. It's a shame we couldn't have paired the foods and drink the way we should have. Your cook is okay, but you may want to hire a professional chef for important parties."

Marie stopped washing the glasses and turned toward Abigail. Her face turned dark but before she could say anything, Megan rushed over and took the glasses from her hand. She pushed them into Abigail's arms and began to usher her out of the room. "Please bring these to the dining room. I'll be there in a minute with the sherry."

When Abigail left, Megan turned back to the kitchen to see Marie with a murderous look on her face. "How dare she? They're lucky they have a place to sleep. Now they go on acting like this is a hotel providing bad service. If you don't call Teddy tomorrow, I'll do it." Marie threw her dishtowel onto the counter and opened the bottle of sherry. "Here, take this out to them. I'll be putting a few things away so they don't spoil and then I'm out of here."

"I'm sorry, Marie. I appreciate all your help. Please don't think I treat you like staff."

"I don't but I've decided I'm going to my own home and bed tonight. If these animals want anything else, tell your father to get his butt out of bed to serve them." Marie thrust the bottle of sherry into Megan's hands and whipped back around to the sink.

Chapter Twenty

Megan walked to the dining room, intent on pulling her father aside and giving him a word or two about his friends. She was in the hall when the shouting began in the dining room, followed by a glass hitting a wall and shattering to the floor.

"What do you mean you don't have the papers, yet?" Kevin shouted at Dean. "Are you saying the entire weekend was an absolute waste? If so, you will certainly come to regret it, Dean."

"Hey, I'm sure our attorney will have everything straightened out by the end of the week, but I won't be able to sign anything until then." Dean offered a large smile in return.

Kevin turned to Randall. "I've got two strip malls closing in Texas. I didn't put both on hold to rush up here to shoot the breeze. I better not lose those deals. The commission alone is worth a few million dollars."

Randall nodded as he put a large Cuban cigar in his mouth and proceeded to light it. After releasing a few puffs of smoke, he waved toward his young partner. "Everything will be fine, boy. Calm down. I'm quite sure Dean would not have lured me all the way to New Jersey unless he knew the estate was free and clear and ready to be sold."

Megan's heart clutched in her chest. She almost dropped the bottle of sherry as it bounced off the sideboard. Abigail rose when she saw Megan enter the room and grabbed at the bottle. "Whew, that was a close call."

"I don't understand what's going on here," Megan said as she turned toward her father. "What do you mean, free and clear?"

"I wanted to surprise you, but Randall and his group are going to buy Misty Manor as well as some of the other parts of the estate."

"What? How could you?" Megan said with fury. "Grandma Rose would be livid if she knew what you were doing."

Dean smirked and said, "Well, then it's good she's not here anymore, isn't it? C'mon, Megan. This place has been falling apart since

Hurricane Sandy, probably even before that. I'm not a homeowner and certainly not able to keep the place going. I'm not interested in patching it up all the time either. I had enough of that when I was a kid. Rose was always worried about one thing or another."

"Billy took care of maintenance over the years and now Tommy has been helping him." Megan stared at her father, daring him to argue.

"Who cares? Besides, it'll be good for the town. Randall wants to build some condos and I hear they're looking at the country club too." Dean nodded toward Randall for support.

"That's right, little lady," Randall said. "We have some work to do, but with the proper makeover, we can turn this house into a private luxury retreat for the upper crust."

"If the sale is legal and the estate is cleared," Kevin said from the other side of the room as he accepted a glass of sherry from Abigail.

"I haven't been given any papers to start reading yet," Savannah said as she took a sip of sherry.

"I don't understand," Megan said. "I don't know exactly what Grandma Rose had in her will, but I got the impression from Teddy it was going to take months."

"What?" Kevin yelled across the room. "I came here ready to finalize the sale." He turned toward Randall. "Did you vet this at all?"

"No, I don't think my friend would try to get one over on me," Randall said with a smile which turned very cold when he turned toward Dean. "Of course, he'd be very sorry if he did."

Abigail sat at the table shaking her head. "I can't believe I'm here listening to this crap. I could be back in Texas, lounging on the lenai, sipping a dry martini." She toasted toward Megan as she spoke. "Not to mention, tonight is card night for my club. We're still playing Texas Hold'em poker, but we got a few new variations."

"At which you are excellent at losing, my dear," Randall said with a smirk toward his wife.

Megan stood and watched the total meltdown as voices, fueled with liquor, continued to rise. Insults and accusations were flung back and forth like a virtual game of volleyball.

She stood in the hall, tears flowing down her cheeks when she heard the knocking on the front door. Shaking she went to the front door and was thrilled when she found Nick on the other side. She flung herself into his arms. Still in uniform, he smiled until he noticed her tears.

As he stepped into the foyer, he asked, "Hey, what's wrong?"

Megan cocked her head toward the dining room. "Take a listen for yourself. Abigail had a boatload of liquor delivered. Now they're all in there arguing about the sale of Misty Manor and turning the rest of the town into a resort and it's awful." Megan let the tears flow as Nick pulled her into a close hug and kissed her. He pulled back after a moment and said, "Let me take care of this."

Walking into the dining room, he listened to the group yelling and threatening each other before he raised his voice and rapped his nightstick against the door frame, loud enough to get their attention. Suddenly, the room was silent. "Excuse me, it's time to break up this little party. Dinner is over, the bar is closed and it's time for you all to move on. Go to bed, watch some TV, your party is over."

The room was silent as the guests simply stared until he heard Abigail say, "For now."

Nick nodded at her. "Good enough for me. Please collect your things and start moving it out of here. I'd appreciate your cooperation."

Megan sauntered into the room and stood at Nick's side as he waited for them to leave the room, nodding at each one as they left. Abigail defiantly stopped at the sideboard and refilled her sherry before she left. Savannah smiled and accidentally brushed against Nick as she passed by.

"I'm on the second floor if you need some company tonight."

Nick chuckled as he squeezed Megan's arm before she could react in the way she desired. "Thanks, I'll keep that in mind, but I'm clearly not interested."

When the guests left the room, Nick helped Megan clear the rest of the dishes and clean the table. They decided to bring the liquor into the kitchen and place it at the back of the counter. As Megan worked with the dishes, Nick massaged the tension out of her neck and shoulders from behind. He then parted her hair and gently leaned forward to place a kiss at the nape of her neck. Megan giggled as Nick's warm breath tickled her. She lifted her hands from the water, grabbed a dishtowel and turned around. "Thank you for helping me out there. You have no idea how much I appreciate you being here tonight."

"I'm more than happy to do so if it means spending time with you," Nick said as he ruffled her hair. "I just wish we could be alone."

"You and me both," Megan agreed. "This is an obnoxious group of people. I can't wait until Teddy gets back so we can straighten everything out."

Nick smiled and immediately yawned. "Sorry, it was such a long shift, I'm exhausted."

"Don't apologize," Megan said. "I'm tired, too."

"I have a suggestion. Why don't we call it a night? We can get together early tomorrow morning for a long quiet walk on the beach and then have some privacy to talk about all this."

Megan smiled. "That sounds like a great idea. What time shall we meet?"

"I'm an early riser, how about seven?"

"Sounds perfect. How about we meet right here in the kitchen, tomorrow morning?"

Nick grabbed the dishtowel out of Megan's hands and threw it on the counter. He guided her toward the hall and turned out the kitchen light as they left the room. "Don't worry about the rest of the dishes. We'll do them when we get back in the morning."

"I won't argue with that," Megan said as she smiled, despite the anxiety snaking up the back of her neck.

Nick grabbed Megan's hand and pulled her up the grand staircase until they were standing on the second-floor landing. Nick pulled her close and planned to give her a kiss goodnight when they heard a noise down the hall. Turning, they saw Abigail making her way from the bathroom toward her room. She looked up, saw them standing together and scowled.

"Do we have hall monitors now?" Abigail said but turned as she heard her husband calling out from the bedroom. Rolling her eyes, she shook her head. "Coming, dear."

Nick suppressed a laugh. "I was going to suggest you visit my room, but I think we should stick with the plan."

"My thoughts, exactly," Megan said as she planted a kiss on his cheek and continued up the grand staircase to her room on the third floor.

Chapter Twenty-One

"Did you sleep well?" Megan asked with a smile when Nick popped into the kitchen the next morning.

"Evidently, better than you did," Nick said as he looked around the room. The dishes were washed and dried. A large pot of coffee was waiting on the counter with cups, cream, sugar, and teaspoons laid out to the side. In the middle of the counter was a platter holding freshly made blueberry muffins and a small container of whipped butter. "What time did you get up?"

"About an hour ago," Megan said as she placed a dish with tea bags next to the coffee pot. "I didn't do all this. Marie came back last night. She said she felt guilty about leaving me with all the dishes so she finished cleaning last night."

"She's a tremendous help around here," Nick said with a nod.

"You're telling me? She's a saint." Megan looked around. "I have no idea what else to leave out."

"Tomato juice, from what I saw of them last night," Nick said. "Maybe some water to hydrate the hangovers."

Megan giggled. "You may be right."

"You have more than enough here now." Nick grabbed her hand. "We have a walk scheduled. It's going to be a beautiful day."

The pair left through the front door, crossed the porch and headed down to the lawn. They made their way to the edge of the boardwalk and began to walk toward town. Megan started to relax and enjoy the day. Years ago, she would get up every morning and walk. Some days she would make a left out the front door and head toward the Point. She would circle the lighthouse and continue to follow the beach into the cove. Other days, she would leave the house and turn right toward the boardwalk. She would walk into town, stop for coffee and return. As long as she completed her two miles every morning, she was happy. Thinking about it, she couldn't believe she hadn't taken a regular walk since she returned to take care of Grandma Rose. Time had flown by and so much had happened, but now she had no excuse not to go each morning. Turning her face toward the beach, she enjoyed the sound of the surf, the laughter of the seagulls and the gentle breeze as it caressed her face.

"Penny for your thoughts?" Megan turned and realized Nick was watching her as they walked.

She shook her head and smiled. "Nothing much. I just realized how much I missed walking every morning. Thank you for suggesting this."

"Excellent way to relax, burn calories and air out your brain," Nick said as he took her hand. "Low impact, too."

The pair continued walking down the boardwalk. They passed the country club which sported gorgeous views of the ocean from its nautical themed dining room. After the country club, the pair walked by a decadent old-fashioned fudge shoppe, a souvenir store selling t-shirts, bathing suits and various other odds and ends and finally a frozen fruit yogurt stand. As they continued to walk, they passed the children's amusement park and two small hotels which fronted the ocean. They were a favorite for tourists and college kids during the summer. Megan paused for a few minutes and looked at the people flowing through the front door.

Nick stopped walking and turned around. "What's up?"

"Nothing, I was just looking at these motels. I'm sure these are the motels that wouldn't allow our lovely guests to check in."

"But the sign in the window says they have a vacancy," Nick said.

"Yes, but it may have been full on Saturday," Megan said. "Today is Monday. I imagine a lot of people are checking out."

"Do you think there's a chance we can suggest they invest in a room?" Nick asked waggling his eyebrows.

"It's worth a shot," Megan said. "We can stress how much more comfortable they'd be here. Closer to town, the shops and restaurants."

"Speaking of restaurants," Nick said, nodding to a café. "Would you like to get a cup of coffee?"

"Sounds great," Megan said as she turned toward the shop. The smell of coffee combined with donuts and pastries was overwhelming when they walked through the door. They walked to the counter and took several minutes to look at the different choices.

"Can I help you?" A woman approached with a smile.

"Hi, I'll have a large vanilla coffee with cream, sugar and cinnamon," Megan said with a smile. The woman looked toward Nick.

"Large coffee, black," Nick said.

"You got it. Can I get you anything else?"

Looking toward each other, Nick grinned. "I'll take a chocolate cream donut." He turned toward Megan. "What about you?"

"Hmm," Megan said, looking at the counter. "I'll have a cinnamon scone."

They chatted while they waited. "It smells so good in here, I could eat twelve things." Nick looked to see what other treats they offered.

"I don't remember this place, but it looks great," Megan said. "I'll bet it's packed on the weekends."

"I'll bet you're right," Nick said as he paid the bill and collected their order. The two walked out onto the boardwalk, found a nice bench and sat down to enjoy their breakfast.

"This is delicious," Megan said as she took a sip of her coffee. "We've got to do this more often." They spent several minutes watching the water. Beachgoers walked onto the sand, carrying chairs, towels and coolers. Off to the side, several people threw bread to the seagulls. Summer lifeguards stepped down onto the beach and began to drag their chairs toward the water.

They looked up to see a teenager in a fluorescent yellow shirt, driving a golf cart down the boardwalk. He stopped at each trashcan and placed a clean bag for use that day. They watched the cart go by and looked up to find Georgie walking directly towards them. She was wearing her traditional red bikini and checking to make sure all the junior lifeguards had shown up for the day.

"Hey, it's great to see you guys down here. I thought you'd forgotten how to get here," Georgie said as she leaned in to give them both a hug.

Megan laughed and looked around. "I guess I did, in a way, but I'm really glad Nick dragged me out here today."

"So am I, honey. You have no idea." Georgie looked over at Nick and winked. She nodded to show her approval. "So, when are we going to get together for some pickup volleyball on the beach?"

"Well, I'd love to sometime soon, but I have a slight problem back at the Manor."

"Oh no, what's going on?" Georgie asked.

"My father blew back into town with that man, Randall Douglas, and he brought some unpleasant friends with him," Megan said with a clouded face. "Last night, they were drinking and discussing their planned purchase of Misty Manor and property."

"Really? What a bastard," Georgie said, placing hands on hips. "I'm sorry. I don't mean to dis your dad, but that's pretty cold."

"You're not saying anything I haven't thought," Megan said. "I can't believe he refused to come back when she was so sick, but he's suddenly here anticipating a windfall."

"He really is a bastard, isn't he?"

"It's worse than that," Megan said. "He's admitted the sooner he sells, the better."

"What? He can't do that, can he?" Georgie asked. "Misty is the oldest Grand Victorian in town. It's been on the Point with the lighthouse for a hundred years. The whole area is a landmark by now. Can't you declare it a historic landmark?"

Megan looked at Nick and shrugged. "Do you think we could do that?"

"We can certainly consider it."

Georgie shifted position and straightened the whistle hanging over her life guard bikini. "What would this new owner want it for?"

Nick cleared his throat and looked at Megan.

"What?" Megan asked when she saw his expression.

"I'm not sure if you overheard him, but the partner, Kevin Shaw, was saying they wanted to redo the house and make it a lavish getaway for executives. They wanted to buy the hotels and make some other changes in the town as well."

Megan fumed. "Over my dead body."

"Not to mention Rose's," Georgie said as she looked at Nick and shrugged. She took Megan's hand. "Seriously, did Rose have a will?"

Megan took a long sip of her coffee. "Yes, she did. I'm trying to get hold of Teddy so we can figure out exactly what's going on."

Georgie knelt on the boardwalk so she was level with Megan's face. "Honey, are you sure you can trust Teddy? Did Rose ever tell you her wishes?"

Megan teared up. "He's been Rose's attorney for years. I grew up with him so I don't think he'd do anything wrong."

"He wouldn't be the first lawyer to take advantage of a large amount of money," Georgie pointed out.

Megan thought for a few moments. "He asked me to sign some papers on Friday. He told me he would call later this week. He definitely didn't want to talk to my father."

"I don't mean to be insulting, but you read everything before you signed it, right?" Georgie asked, concern written on her face.

Megan looked down at her coffee, then back at her friends. "Not really. I read the first page but it was thirty pages of legalese. He did say Rose left me something in the will."

Nick slid close to Megan and placed his arm around her shoulders. "Assuming that's true, how do you know you didn't sign eighty percent of your inheritance over to him? The fact that he's waiting for a while may be all he needs to file the documents. Did he leave copies of anything?"

Megan shook her head. "No, he didn't leave me anything." Megan's hands started to shake. "What if I just made the biggest mistake of my life? I trusted him. I can't believe I would be that stupid."

"Do you think he could be working with your father in any way?" Nick asked as he wadded up his napkin and threw it in the trashcan next to the bench.

"I don't think so. He wanted to run when he saw Dean. Storm and all, he couldn't wait to leave. Dean said they had a lot to talk about, but Teddy blew him off. If those two are working together, they deserve an award for their acting skills."

Megan looked over at Nick. "What do you think I should do?"

Nick returned a half-hearted smile and tried to be supportive. He didn't want to upset Megan any more than she was but he shared her concerns. "Listen, let's walk back on the beach. We can work these donuts off. When we get back to the house, we'll call Teddy. He may call back faster if I leave my name."

Georgie jumped up. "That sounds like a great plan." She looked over at Megan. "Please, promise me you'll call me later and let me know how you are. I don't care what we do, but we have to get together this week."

Megan nodded her head. "I will."

"I'm serious. Lifeguards go off at five. I'm free this week, so call me."

Megan smiled as she stood up and leaned in for a hug. "Thanks, Georgie. We'll talk later, I hope," Megan thought as her mind wandered to Teddy once more.

Chapter Twenty-Two

"I can't believe I could be so stupid, I really trusted Teddy," Megan said as they walked along the ocean edge. Water flowed around their ankles as the waves rushed in to shore. They had taken off their shoes and wiggled their toes in the wet sand. The water was cool at first, but had warmed quickly as they walked. "But Rose trusted him, so that's why I thought I should trust him too."

Nick nodded as he considered her logic. "True and we'll find out soon enough. If it's something you don't agree with, you can hire another lawyer and hang them up in court for years."

Megan frowned. "As long as those people leave the house." Megan stopped walking, looked over at Nick and smiled. "Thank you for dragging me out for a walk today. Despite all the confusion, I think this has been the best morning since I came back to New Jersey."

Nick wrapped his arms around Megan's waist and drew her to him. She looked up as he bent his head for a lip-crushing kiss. Megan felt her stomach tighten and was glad Nick was holding her. She hadn't felt tingling like that since she was in high school. He pulled back and placed his forehead against hers as the waves continued to crash against the side of their bodies. "Not a bad start to the day, that's for sure."

Megan laughed, then suddenly leaned down and splashed water at Nick. "Hey!" He began to chase her as she ran further into the ocean. Her flowing white skirt became wet with ocean water. The pair ran back and forth until they found themselves deep enough to dive under the water. They continued to dodge waves, swim and laugh until Nick caught Megan in a full body embrace. As much as they enjoyed clinging to each other, Nick was concerned when he felt Megan start to shiver. "We better get home and dry off." He released her from his grasp and they started back toward Misty Manor.

"Thank you for a great morning," Megan said as she held Nick's hand.

"My pleasure," Nick said as he smiled. "It's been a great morning for me too."

The two walked in silence for a few moments when Megan stopped and pointed to the sky. "Hey Nick, look at all those birds."

"I see them. There must be something on the beach."

"It looks like they're right across from Misty Manor," Megan said as she picked up the pace.

"Nothing was going on when we left this morning." Nick quickened his step to keep up with Megan.

"The weather has been terrible the last few days," Megan said. "I hope a dolphin didn't wash up on the beach."

"We're too far away to know what's happened."

"Let's get over there," Megan said, becoming agitated. "If it's a dolphin and it's still alive, we have a chance at saving its life."

"Okay, I'm ready," Nick teased as he took off at a slight jog.

"Very funny," Megan puffed as she now chased him. "You just wait. In a couple of months, you'll be struggling to keep up with me."

Nick laughed as he jogged and slowed down as they approached the beach sitting directly across from Misty Manor. He bent forward and let himself enjoy a few deep breaths while placing his hands on his knees.

Megan caught up to him and stopped. "Wow, I really have to start exercising more. Maybe I can meet up with Georgie for her morning runs. I hear the lifeguards have a killer workout."

Nick laughed. "You're not the only one, my love, but enough of that. Look at those birds. They're definitely hovering over something Maybe, it's a school of fish."

"I don't know about that, Nick. Look at that big lump of seaweed," Megan said as she pointed straight ahead. "Maybe a poor dolphin got tangled up in a net and the birds are just waiting to pounce."

"Let's go check it out," Nick said. "Maybe we can help."

Nick grabbed Megan's hand and quickly ran toward the pile of seaweed.

"We'd have to cut the net and pull the dolphin out toward shallow water. The waves can do the rest," Megan said as she noticed the knot forming at the base of her stomach. "I hope it's not too late."

"Let's just get there." Nick grunted as he continued across the sand.

Megan felt a sudden spurt of energy and ran ahead. "I'm going to beat you," Megan shouted as she got closer to the clump.

Nick followed behind but froze when he heard her blood curdling scream.

"Megan what's wrong?" Nick yelled as he scanned the horizon. He saw Megan standing over the lump of seaweed, one hand clutching her stomach, her other hand on her head. Picking up speed, he reached her side within several seconds. He placed his arm around her and pulled her close. *What the hell was going on?*

"Oh my," Megan said as she sobbed and pointed toward the seaweed.

Holding her to his side, he said, "What is it? Is it a dolphin? It's okay, Megan. The police get calls all the time for things washing up on the beach."

"But you don't understand," Megan cried as she grabbed on to Nick.

"What?" Nick asked as he grew frustrated. "I've seen a lot of sea life wash up on the beach."

Megan tried to explain. "Nick, I see an eye, but it's not a dolphin eye."

"What are you talking about?" Nick asked as he tried to understand.

They stood near the pile of seaweed. She turned toward Nick and clearly looked as if she may vomit at any moment and grabbed his arm for support.

"Are you okay?"

"Nick, I saw his eye," Megan said as she started to become seriously unfocused.

"Okay, whose eye?" Nick asked as he tried to look around Megan.

"It's wide open and staring through the seaweed," Megan tried to explain. Nick grabbed her hands to stop the trembling.

"Calm down. I don't know what's going on," Nick said. He grabbed her by the shoulders and looked her in the face. "Stay here, don't move. Let me get closer to check it out."

Megan nodded silently as she turned to face Misty Manor. She didn't watch as Nick ran toward the large pile of seaweed as it crashed against the jetty with every wave. Nick pulled some of the seaweed back but jumped as he realized there was a body underneath the kelp. He immediately knelt in the water and tried to find a pulse. Finding none, he grabbed his cell phone from his pocket, dialed 911 and called in the report. Replacing his phone, he grabbed the body under the arms and dragged it to the edge of the water. He attempted to drain water from the lungs. Nick immediately reached down and tried once again to find a pulse. He noticed the bloated face, the lifeless eyes, small bites on the nose and cheeks and knew this man had been dead for a while.

The sound of sirens filled the air as Nick blew out a deep breath. He knew the beach would be packed with activity in just a few moments. He did a quick survey of the body to look for any trauma. Shark bites usually meant missing limbs and blood loss, but all the extremities were intact and if any bleeding had occurred, it would have stopped long ago.

Engrossed in his exam, he didn't hear Megan sneak up behind him despite the sniffles as tears streamed down her face. She dropped to her knees beside him, then quickly raced to the ocean and vomited in the water. Nick was torn between going to her side and staying with the body as he had been trained to do. He stood and called out to her. "Are you okay?"

Megan nodded as she looked back and wiped her hair away from her face. She slowly walked toward him without looking at the bloated corpse lying on the sand. Emergency personnel started running onto the beach. They carried safety float equipment as well as medical bags and a stretcher. Megan's head spun until she was pulled away by her friend Georgie. "Come over here, sweetie. Let the professionals do their job."

Megan turned away from the scene and placed the back of her head against Nick's shoulder as Georgie stroked her arm. Confused, Megan asked, "Georgie, what are you doing here?"

"I manage the Misty Point lifeguards. I get called for all beach emergencies." Megan simply nodded as Nick wrapped his arms around her. Georgie continued to comfort her as she watched the emergency responders try to revive the body with no luck. Several officers crowded around when they were called over by the crew who stopped compressions, realizing too much time had lapsed.

Georgie looked back at Megan. "Are you better now?" When Megan shook her head, Georgie continued to press. "Did you recognize him?"

Megan continued to nod as she whispered in a hoarse voice. "Yes. It's Randall Douglas."

Chapter Twenty-Three

Megan sat on the sand and stared out at the water. The last several hours had gone by in slow motion. The group watched while the medical examiner and crime scene unit were called to examine the body.

Nick gave Megan a squeeze and nodded at Georgie. Wondering what the medical examiner thought of the beach drowning, Nick walked across the sand to talk to his boss, Chief Davis. As he approached, Davis turned and raised an eyebrow.

"This is the second body we've found at Misty Manor within the past few months. It's starting to be a common occurrence," Davis said as he shielded his eyes.

"C'mon Chief, you know this was an accident," Nick defended.

Davis looked at the scene before him. "Not so sure about that, Nick."

"Why? What did they find to call everyone down here? Was he shot?"

"Not that I'm aware of," Davis scowled.

"Then what?"

"Where were you last night?"

"Really?" Nick asked in disbelief. "You're going there?"

Davis gestured to the cops standing on the beach. "Some of the guys said you've been staying here. They also said you've been getting mighty cozy with Ms. Stanford lately."

Nick scowled. "Maybe they ought to think about minding their own business."

"Help me out here. If you don't give me something, I'm going to have to start grilling your girlfriend over there and it doesn't look like it would be an appropriate time for her. Besides, there's plenty of chatter around town, most of it crap. I trust you wouldn't lie to me, Nick. So, what's the story."

Nick sighed and crossed his arms across his chest. He looked Davis straight in the eye. "Look, this is what I know so far. Friday afternoon, Megan was here taking care of a little business. I had been calling her, since she was so distraught over Rose's passing. Her friends and I have been trying to get her out of the house."

"Very noble of you, Nick," Davis said with a smirk.

"Screw off. Anyway, from what I was told, her deadbeat father suddenly shows up with this guy in tow. It seems they spent the afternoon in town, pissing people off. They needed a place to stay so they show up unannounced at Misty Manor."

"I've heard rumors, but tell me who the hell he is."

"He's supposedly a big time real estate developer from Texas. Buys property and turns some of them into luxury getaways and builds those communities of cookie cutter houses. The only thing the owner chooses is the outside color."

"Based on the chatter, it sounds like he had a bad reputation and certainly wasn't welcome when he showed up."

"Neither was Dean Stanford," Nick spat. "The ass can't come home to check on his own mother or make the funeral, but beats it home when he smells a buck in the making."

Davis looked up and watched a small crowd collecting on the porch of Misty Manor. He nodded toward the house. "So, who are all those people?"

Nick half turned to see who had gathered. "That's his entourage, except for Marie." He looked at Chief Davis. "You know Marie O'Sullivan from town. Anyway, Saturday morning, I pulled Megan out of the house to have breakfast. When we got back, these people were camped on the steps of the front porch. The guy is Douglas's business partner, the older woman his wife and the younger woman his assistant. Dean Stanford is the one hanging back." Nick continued to scan the beach. "Everyone else hanging around has morbid curiosity, although I wonder if Billy is watching from the Point. He may have seen something."

"Good catch," Davis said. "I'll send someone up there to talk to him. He never leaves the lighthouse."

"Okay, now that I just did half your job, tell me why there's so much activity here. What did they find?"

"I can't tell you much, Nick. With you being so close to Megan, we're verging on a conflict of interest here, but I will tell you Mr. Douglas appears to have a particular type of head wound."

"His body kept washing up against the jetty."

"It's not that type of head wound. It looks deliberate. The ME is gonna take him back to the morgue. The autopsy will tell us if he drowned."

Nick nodded for the moment, deep in thought.

"You know I'm going to have to question everyone up there," Davis said, carefully watching Nick.

Nick looked at Davis and shrugged. "Hey, do what you gotta do. You may find some interesting stories."

"What about notification? How's the wife gonna take it?"

"Based on what I saw last night, I don't think it'll be too much of a problem."

"Why do you say that?"

"Megan can give you a better picture, but it sounds like the honeymoon has been over for quite some time in that marriage, if you know what I mean."

Davis stared at the porch for a moment. "Okay, we'll see how she reacts. Remember, not a word of this to anyone. Right?"

"Can I sit in on the notification?"

Davis turned toward Nick. "Why would you want to do that?"

"I'm just as curious as you are," Nick said. "As far as I know, there's nothing criminal about finding a body."

"I'll think about it," Davis said. "Why don't you gather the masses up at the house? Don't let on about anything. Let us clean up down here and then we'll be up to take some statements and such."

"You got it," Nick said. "I'll try to keep them together."

"Appreciate it," Davis said as he gave a curt nod. "Nick, I'm depending on you."

Chapter Twenty-Four

Holding her hand, Nick escorted Megan up the porch steps. They were greeted by several voices at once. "Hey, what's going on down there? The police wouldn't let us on the beach."

Nick held his hands up. "Everyone just relax and stay calm. Why don't we all go inside and take a seat in the parlor?"

"I can't find Randall."

No one moved, instead they turned to see Abigail grab one of the porch posts. She scanned the beach and choked back a sob. "Is it Randall? I can't find him."

Marie approached Abigail and tried to hug her around the shoulders. Nick turned back and said, "I'm not sure who it is or what's going on. They wouldn't let me near."

Nick glanced at Megan to make sure she remained quiet as he had instructed her on the way to the house.

"I just know it's him. It must be Randall. The man never could swim." Abigail swallowed hard but seemed suspiciously composed.

Within minutes, Chief Davis approached the Grand Victorian and proceeded to walk up the porch steps. His visage was blank. He wore his game face well. Davis kept it that way to ensure he didn't give away any information. His goal was to gather info and watch for reactions.

Davis stopped when he reached the top stair. He took a moment to look everyone in the eye. They stared at him intently, looking for a twitch or a tell as to what he was thinking. He took off his hat and held it at his side. "Morning, folks." He half turned toward the beach and pointed. "As you can see, we've had a bit of a tragedy this morning. I hate to take your time but I need to have you all gather inside so I can talk to you one by one. I prefer you don't talk to each other in the meantime." He looked at Nick and said, "Maybe you could help me with that."

"What are you talking about?" Kevin asked, indignation in his voice. "What happened down there? Are we suspects?"

"I was thinking more like witnesses," Davis said. "But since you brought it up, what do you think you'd be a suspect for?"

"How the hell do I know? I don't know what's going on." Kevin pointed to the beach, his face turning red with rage.

"Then, let's go inside and start over." Davis walked to the front door, paused and gestured for everyone else to walk in before him. The small group of people obliged and one by one passed him as they entered the foyer and headed into the parlor.

Davis held Megan back as she attempted to pass him near the door. "Excuse me, do you have a private room I can meet with your guests in? I'd like to talk to each one alone."

Megan paused for a moment and then nodded her head. "Of course, let me show you the library. You'll have privacy in there."

"Thank you," Davis said as he crossed the threshold and closed the front door. He followed her as she led him to the formal library of Misty Manor. She used a key to open the door and walk into the room. He followed her and looked around. The air was stuffy and a few of the side tables held a good bit of dust. Looking toward the window, he saw a number of fine particles floating in a shaft of sunlight falling toward the floor.

They crossed to the large mahogany desk and Megan pulled out the chair. "You can sit here if you want."

"Thank you," Davis said as he pulled the chair around to the other side. "I 'd prefer to sit up close so I can watch their reaction."

Megan watched him and simply nodded at his logic.

"Whatever you think is best."

"Let's go back to the parlor and I'll ask Mrs. Douglas to join me," Davis said as he pointed the way. The two left the library and crossed the hall to the parlor to find the small group seated there. Expectantly, they all looked up as the pair approached, anxiety set in their eyes. Davis looked around the room until his gaze landed on Abigail Douglas. "Please ma'am, I'd like to speak to you first."

Chapter Twenty-Five

Davis brought Abigail into the library and offered her one of the chairs near the desk. "I'm sorry to have to do this but I need to ask a few questions," Davis said as he pulled his pad out of his pocket. Would you mind giving me your name?" He waited for a few seconds and then looked at Abigail when she didn't answer.

"Please, let's skip the pleasantries, Chief. Is it Randall?" Abigail's eyes were wide in her pale face.

"We don't have an official identification yet," Davis said. He pulled his phone from another pocket and searched for an app. "I'd like to know if you can identify this card. We found it in a wallet with the deceased." Opening his photo app, he showed Abigail a photo of a driver's license. "Does this look familiar, ma'am?"

Abigail leaned forward to get a better look at the photo. She immediately recognized the Texas driver's license and let out a gasp. The card was faded and obviously dated, but it was his.

Davis tried to have her focus. Notifications were difficult as it was and worse when a family member lost focus, immediately asking themselves hundreds of questions. *What was the last thing I said to him? Did he suffer? Who did he think of at the last moment? What was the last thing he ate? What happens now?* Davis had the same questions, but for different reasons.

"Ma'am, I know it's difficult, but I'd like you to look at this photo again. Can you confirm the spelling of the name and the birthdate?" Abigail looked again and slowly nodded.

"Is that your correct address?"

"Yes, that's correct," Abigail said.

Davis noted her voice was steady although her hands were shaking. She swallowed hard, but she wasn't crying anymore.

"Did you both reside there?"

"What kind of a question is that, Sheriff?"

"Actually, it's Chief Davis," he said as he nodded. "Sorry, Ma'am, I need to confirm the information for the police report. You understand."

Abigail shot him an icy stare for a few moments, then relented. "Of course. Yes, that is our address. We have been married for thirty-five blissful years."

"Ma'am, do you think you could look at a photo for me? It's a bit shocking but you may be able to help us with identification."

Abigail's face grew still as she swallowed. "I suppose I can, if that's what I have to do."

Chief Davis hit an app on his phone to bring up a photo and turned it back toward Abigail. "Is this your husband?"

Abigail immediately covered her mouth with her hand. Shocked, she stifled a sob and absently nodded.

Davis was silent for a moment as she composed herself. "I'm sorry for your loss." He noticed she calmed herself rather quickly, but grief was funny that way. One moment the bereaved were shocked and the next they were angry. Denial and rage took over as families tried to control an uncontrollable situation.

"When was the last time you saw your husband?"

Abigail shifted uncomfortably. "Last night, in bed, of course."

Davis looked up and nodded, his expression blank. He didn't have exact details and would wait for the coroner to offer those, but they all agreed Mr. Randall Douglas had probably been floating in the ocean for at least twelve hours.

"What time did the two of you get up this morning?" Davis had his pen poised, ready to record her answer on his pad. He watched her face work as she struggled to answer the question. She swallowed, looked down at her hands and shrugged.

"He was gone when I got up this morning," she said. "I don't know when he got up."

Davis nodded and cleared his throat. "Did you sense him turning over in bed or getting up to use the bathroom sometime during the night?"

"No," Abigail said and shook her head. "I was in a very deep sleep, so I have no idea what he did. I'm pretty sure he was there when I went to bed."

"Pretty sure?" Davis asked. "You're not positive he was there? Did you say goodnight?"

Abigail clenched her jaw as her anger began to build. "He was in the bedroom while I was down the hall, in the bathroom, getting ready for bed. I heard him calling for me as I started walking back."

"What time was that?" Davis cocked his head.

"I don't remember, exactly," Abigail said as she looked around the room.

"I understand you're upset, but you seem to be having trouble remembering details from last night."

Abigail's head snapped around. "Listen, Ranger Davis, or whatever you're called in New Jersey, I've been in this hell hole for forty eight hours. My husband made us rush up here. As a result, I have been stuck in a house without decent food or rooms while he was off playing in Atlantic City."

Davis was now interested, taking notes as she spoke. When she stopped, he prompted her. "And?"

"And last night, I'd had enough. I found a liquor store and had them make a delivery. So, the reason I don't remember much is because I'd had a few drinks before I went to bed. We all did and that's a small compensation for being stuck here."

"I see," Davis said. "But you remember him calling you in the hall?"

"Yes, he definitely called out when I was in the hall. I remember because it annoyed me."

Davis closed his pad and placed his pen in his pocket. "That's enough for now, Mrs. Douglas. I'm sorry you're having such a tough time here, but it'll be a few more days. The medical examiner must complete an autopsy and we need to close our investigation before I can release the body. Please do not leave Misty Manor until you clear it with us. We'll probably have more questions for you."

"Investigation? Am I a suspect or something?"

"Why would I think you're a suspect?" Davis asked.

"That's what I'd like to know," Abigail asked. "The man never could swim. If the damn fool tried, it's no wonder he drowned."

Chapter Twenty-Six

"Nick, what's going on?" Megan whispered as she sidled up to Nick in the parlor. She leaned against his shoulder to garner strength. "What did they find?"

Nick looked at her and smiled. He leaned over and whispered, "Let's just say, something doesn't look right. The injuries aren't consistent with a typical drowning."

"Are you kidding me?"

Nick laid a hand on her arm. "Listen, we don't know anything yet. The medical examiner has to complete the autopsy, but something funny showed up. Davis has to get statements now before everyone has a chance to concoct a cover story."

"You think someone here did it?" Megan asked. "There's a murderer in the house?" Megan began to look around the room. Kevin Shaw sat on the couch, angrily thumbing through his phone. Savannah Williams stood by the picture window looking at the beach. Megan could see a flurry of activity beyond the window and she groaned as she watched the police stretch yellow crime scene tape across an expanse of the beach. The police had done the same exact thing a couple of months ago when she moved back to Misty Manor and decided to knock down the cottages which had been damaged in Hurricane Sandy. The demolition had gone well until a dead body turned up in the debris.

Megan looked toward the hall and spied Marie carrying a pitcher of iced tea into the parlor. When she caught Marie's attention, Megan raised her eyebrows. Marie shrugged back. She placed the pitcher on the coffee table and left glasses as well. Not knowing what else to do, she sat on one of the couches and nervously fumbled with her hands.

The group turned toward the doorway as Dean Stanford swept in the room. He was dressed in jeans and a dirty sweatshirt. In his hand, he held a glass full of scotch on the rocks. As he gestured with his hand, the golden liquor slopped over the rim of the glass and dripped onto the wooden floor. "What in the hell is going on here?"

Megan turned red with embarrassment as she watched her father make a jerk of himself. Just as she prepared to say something to her father, they heard a loud noise coming from the library. Angry voices could be heard through the wall. Megan turned toward Nick. "I can't hear what they're saying, can you?"

Nick shook his head. "No, and I don't want to, but it sounds like Abigail is giving Davis a tough time."

"That's not exactly grieving widow behavior, is it?"

"How do we know she's actually grieving? By the way, your father doesn't look like he's overly upset at losing his good friend either, does he?"

"It's hard to get upset when you only think of yourself," Megan said as she made a derisive sound.

The group looked up when they heard the door of the library open. Abigail burst out of the room with Davis following behind. She tossed her head and marched across the hall toward the parlor but stopped short when she saw Dean standing there with a drink in his hand.

"Where did you get that?" Abigail asked angrily as she looked at Dean.

Dean looked back at Abigail and blinked. He then looked down at the glass in his hand and smiled. "I found everything in the kitchen. That's where they stashed all the liquor." Dean giggled as he looked at Abigail.

"That's my liquor," Abigail said angrily. "They can't hide it from me. I paid for it."

"Then I suggest you go fetch a glass for yourself," Dean said as he half toasted her with his glass.

"That's exactly what I plan to do," Abigail said as she spun on her heel and marched off toward the kitchen.

Chapter Twenty-Seven

Chief Davis stood in the hall and watched Abigail walk off. He scanned the room and nodded to Megan's father. "Mr. Stanford, my sympathies regarding your mother."

Dean smiled inappropriately and took a swig of scotch. "Thanks, Davis. I see you've done well for yourself. You've gotten a promotion."

Davis nodded his head. "Yes, I've recently been promoted to Chief of the Misty Point Police Department."

"Well, that's very special," Dean said as he nodded his head.

"Yes, and as Chief of the Police Department, I'll need to speak with you for a few moments about the death of Randall Douglas."

"Me, why me?" Dean asked.

"We have to take a statement from everyone," Davis said. "He was found right outside Misty Manor. We need to establish a time line."

Dean stood in the hall, holding his drink and gave Officer Davis a blank look.

"Mr. Stanford, would you please join me in the library?" Davis said in frustration as he nodded toward the library to encourage Dean to move. He then threw Nick a guarded look to show his displeasure at the feigned cooperation he had received so far.

The two men entered the room and Dean immediately took a seat behind the desk. He slapped his almost empty rocks glass on the desk and splashed amber liquid on the blotter. Laughing he said, "Good thing, I didn't get any of that on the wood. My mother would have had a fit if I left a ring on this desk, but she's not here to harp on me anymore, is she?"

"Perhaps she liked to preserve fine things," Davis said as he sat in a chair on the opposite side of the desk and watched Dean with a curious stare. He noted the man's lack of respect to his family and his home. "I know things were difficult for you and your family when your father went missing, but I'm sure Rose tried her best. She was a sweet, generous woman and supported you and most of this community for years."

Dean looked up at Davis, hatred in his eyes. He snorted a laugh. "Ha and because of that I was always expected to be exactly like my mother. Generous, kind, loving, gracious and people expected even more from me. Do you have any friggin' idea what that's like? You're living under a microscope everyday of your life. You can't even curse in public without people being disappointed in your behavior. Meanwhile, you're getting your ass kicked in school. All the kids hated me because my family had money and owned most of the town. They claimed every achievement I made in school was because of who I was, not because of what I knew." Dean mumbled, shook his head and squeezed his glass tightly. "I finally said *screw this* and did what I wanted." He picked up his glass, threw the last drops of scotch down his throat and slapped his glass on the desk. He began to stand, "I need another drink."

"Not yet," Davis said. He nodded to the chair and silently commanded him to sit back down. "I have a few questions to ask and I want you to be coherent enough to answer them." Davis knew these answers could be thrown out with any good lawyer, but Dean's loosened tongue may provide more answers.

"Randall Douglas was a friend of yours?" Davis asked as he took out his pad and pen.

"Yeah, I guess you could say that. We had some fun times."

"Where and when did you meet?"

Dean pursed his lips and thought for a moment. "Years ago, he was a friend of a college buddy of mine. I met him at a party, throwing around that big Texas drawl of his. He got a lot of crap because of it." Dean laughed at the memory.

"You stayed in touch?"

"You know, money attracts money. People stay in touch."

"Actually, I don't," Davis said as he thought about how hard he and many others worked to pay bills and keep a roof over their head.

"We both enjoyed a taste for good cigars, aged liquor and expensive steak. We would cross paths from time to time."

"It's interesting you happened to cross paths just after Rose died," Davis pointed out.

Dean leaned forward and placed his arms on the desk. "Let's stop the games. We both know it wasn't coincidence Randall and I got together and we both know I have no love for this house or this town."

Or your mother, Davis thought.

"But obviously, there's a ton of money in play here. A lot of it is tied up in Misty Manor and the property my mother owned. I'm sure you already know Randall was a large real estate developer with a ton of contacts. He'd been watching this place for a while, but we knew Rose would never sell while she was alive. Randall called me after Hurricane Sandy. He was hoping he could pick up a lot of real estate for a song but she refused to even consider the idea. So, he said he would wait her out and that's what he did. Unfortunately, the man goes swimming at night and now I'm screwed out of that deal." Dean shook his head. "No matter, I'm sure there'll be other contractors interested in this place and I haven't had a chance to talk to his partner yet either."

Davis swallowed at the audacity of the man before him. He had met narcissistic men before but never one this cold.

"When was the last time you saw Mr. Douglas?"

Dean rubbed his temples. "Yesterday, at dinner. We were eating and there was a shouting match. Your buddy, Nick, came in and broke it up, sent everyone to bed." Dean made invisible quote marks in the air to emphasize his disdain at being told what to do.

Davis kept a straight face but made a mental note to have a lengthy discussion with Nick about the events at Misty Manor over the weekend.

"Did you go to your room?"

"I did at first, but then I sort of had a date, so I went out."

Davis raised his eyebrows in surprise. "Oh really? So, someone can confirm your whereabouts last night?"

"I guess so," Dean said, getting angry. "But why the hell would they need to? I thought the man drowned. I didn't realize I was a suspect in anything."

"Just getting some facts," Davis said with a friendly smile and a shrug. "There's a ton of paperwork with any unplanned death. You know how it is."

Dean clenched his teeth. "Are we almost done here? I really need another scotch."

"Just a few more questions. When did you both arrive in Misty Point?"

"We flew in Friday, but we went to Atlantic City for the weekend. We got back here yesterday."

"Anything unusual happen this weekend? Was Mr. Douglas upset about anything?"

Dean grinned and shook his head. "I see what you're getting at. You think he committed suicide?"

"Just collecting facts, that's all," Davis said as he pointed to his book.

"No, he seemed fine. We had an exciting time. As a matter of fact, he called his partner, wife and assistant up here because he wanted to get moving on this project."

"Why did they need to be here for that?"

"He wanted them to see New Jersey. Apparently, his partner and wife need to sign off on all the paperwork and the assistant handles the rest."

"I see," Davis said.

"What I see is my deal disappearing in a nuclear meltdown," Dean said as he got up from his chair. "Sorry, Davis, but I can't think anymore." Dean picked up his glass and walked out of the room in search of his next scotch.

Chapter Twenty-Eight

"Hello? Is anyone here?" The young officer stopped pounding the door and took a step backward to look for activity.

"Hold your horses. I'm coming," Billy Conklin shouted down the stairs of the Misty Point Lighthouse. Billy had been taking care of the lighthouse for approximately fifty-five years. His sharp eye had recently helped to stop an attempt on Megan's life, which had been his mission for staying in Misty Point all along. After George Stanford went missing, he stayed in the lighthouse and kept watch over Misty Manor, Rose and the family. The lantern room of the lighthouse had a magnificent view of most of the beach and some of the town. In addition to keeping watch, Billy also kept up the house as much as he could for Rose, and called only on his nephew, Tommy McDonough, when he needed help.

"I'm eighty years old, you know. These bones don't move as fast as they used to," Billy said as he opened the door to let the officer in. True to his reputation of being cranky, he looked at the officer. "What do you want?"

Holding back a smile, Officer Peters nodded his head. "Hey Billy, how are you?"

"Oh, you know my name?"

"Yes, we met a month ago at Misty Manor."

Billy took a moment and looked the young officer up and down. "Well, I can't say I remember you, but I don't remember most things these days anyway."

"Well, I'm hoping you're going to remember something from last night."

"Like what?" Billy asked as he looked at his guest while he squinted his right eye.

"A body washed up near the beach today," Peters began.

"Yeah, I've been watching all you fellas crawling around down there."

"The crime scene unit is there right now."

"What are they doing there? I thought you said the man drowned," Billy asked with a scowl.

"Billy, we need to decide if this was an accident or something else. We don't know where he went into the water. I'm here to ask you if you were keeping watch last night."

"You know I was, boy," Billy said with a disgusted look.

"Well then, did you see anyone on the beach last night?" Peters watched his face carefully while waiting for the answer.

Billy reached up and scratched the back of his grey crewcut head. "I saw a few people last night. The weather kept a lot of people off the beach, but there's always some that don't heed the warnings."

"Was the water rough last night, Billy?"

"You know it was, boy," Billy said. "Been rough all week with these storms. Windy with rain on and off, but at least it's fairly warm."

"Who did you see?"

"Always a couple of people walking the sand, crossing the Point and watching the moon. It was a full moon last night. That's why the water was so high and the waves rough."

"Who else did you see Billy?"

"Just two people standing by the jetty." Billy turned around and headed back to his room.

"Where are you going?" Peters asked. "I had a few more questions."

Billy looked back at the officer. "I told you I'm eighty years old, boy. You may be able to stand here and talk all day, but I got bad knees, hips and my back hurts. If you want to talk to me, you're gonna have to follow me. I've gotta sit down or my legs are going to give out." Billy slowly limped down the stone passage, his right hand holding onto the wall as he went. He sidled around the entryway of a room and plopped down in a rocking chair.

Peters followed him into the room. "You okay?"

Taking a moment to catch his breath, he said, "I am now."

"You still working this place all by yourself?" Peters asked as he looked around the room.

"For the most part," Billy said. "Tommy stops by as much as he can. He's a good boy. He helps me with the lighthouse when I need it."

"I'm glad to hear that," Peters said as he pulled up a nearby stool. "So, can you tell me more about last night? You mentioned two people by the jetty?"

"What about them?" Billy asked.

"Did you see anything specific? What time was it last night?"

Billy paused for a moment. "It was getting near 11pm."

"You sure?"

"Of course, I'm sure, boy. I know how to read time. I watch the stars every night." Billy gestured with his right hand at the officer.

"Okay, I believe you," Office Peters said. "What do you think they were doing?"

"I told you. They were standing by the jetty."

"Were they talking, kissing, hugging, fighting?"

Billy looked up and rubbed his stubbled cheek for a moment. "They didn't look like they were necking. One was bigger than the other, but I'm not sure if they were a couple." Billy shrugged. "Could be two guys, two girls, or one of each for all I know."

"Are you sure it was only two people?

"Far as I know, I can still count past two," Billy growled.

"Were they holding anything? Did they have a blanket or sit on the sand?"

Waiting several moments, Billy finally answered. "They had something with glass with them."

Peters looked up to watch Billy's face. "How do you know they had glass? It was dark last night."

"That's exactly how I know," Billy crossed his arms and nodded as if to say, *Why is this so hard to understand?*

"I'm sorry, Billy. How does that help you?"

Billy huffed as if he were about to teach a stupid kid an important lesson. "I'm in a lighthouse. The light constantly burns and turns, you know what I mean?" When Officer Peters didn't respond, Billy continued. "Each time the light was focused toward the jetty, I saw a reflection from whatever it was. I doubt anyone was using a mirror last night, so the next thing would be glass. It doesn't always work that way, but it could be."

"Did you hear anything? Voices perhaps? Did you hear laughter or shouting?"

"Only thing I heard from up here was the wind whipping around the Point," Billy said. "I can hear the waves crashing on the shore but not always. It depends on the conditions."

Billy yawned and scratched the side of his chest. "Getting a bit weary, boy."

"Okay, one more question," Officer Peters said. "I appreciate you taking time with me."

"Did I have a choice? You didn't make that clear when you got here," Billy said as he stared at the officer.

Officer Peters chuckled. "Guess not."

"Okay, get it over with, ask your question."

"Did you see anything happen? Did you see one of them fall or try to dive in the water?"

"That's two and a half questions," Billy pointed out. "See, I told you I could count past two. The answer to that is, no. One time I looked and there they were. Next time I looked, they were gone."

Officer Peters stood up, leaned forward and shook his hand. "Okay, thanks for talking to me. You've been a tremendous help."

"I have? I'll be darned if I know anything important," Billy shrugged in response. "Do you mind going to the door yourself. My leg is bothering me today."

"No problem. Stay healthy, Billy." Peters turned, made his way to the hall, down the stairs, and out the front door realizing the timeline had just been set.

Chapter Twenty-Nine

Davis looked around the parlor of Misty Manor. Kevin was still on the couch. Savannah was slowly taking in the contents of the parlor by examining the items on the shelves of the bookcase and the trinkets on the table near the front window. Abigail had returned with a water glass filled with ice and scotch. She sat in the corner rubbing her head while she sipped from the glass. Across the room, Dean Stanford slouched in an easy chair. Davis looked to his left where he saw Nick and Megan sitting on a settee on the side of the room while Marie was now standing by the door. No one appeared to be overly distraught at the death of Mr. Randall Douglas.

Davis nodded at Nick and then walked over to the couch. "Mr. Shaw? Would you please join me in the library?"

Kevin looked up with a scowl as his smart phone rattled off a small bing. Kevin looked down, quickly read the message and hurriedly tapped away in response. Once he sent the message, he looked up and nodded to Davis. "I hope this doesn't take too long." He kept talking as they walked. "I was a busy man to begin with but now that Randall has checked out, I'm a very busy man."

Davis pulled a chair out for him. "Yes, I'm sorry for your loss. Would you please have a seat?"

When Kevin had situated himself, Davis sat in the chair opposite him. He made a show of taking out his pad and pen. "I'd like to ask you a few questions about Mr. Douglas and your business."

"That normally involves the board of directors and our attorneys," Kevin said. He pulled at his trouser and crossed his leg to display his annoyance at the interview.

"I appreciate that," Davis said tightly "but perhaps you can simplify some information for a small-town beach cop such as myself."

"I could try," Kevin huffed. "How did this happen?"

"That's exactly what we're trying to determine," Davis said.

"Why are you asking us? You saw the body. Did he drown? Did he slip? What happened?"

"We're not quite sure, which is why the medical examiner will have to do an autopsy."

Kevin scowled and looked at his watch. His text messages were pinging on both his phone and the watch he wore on his wrist which distracted him each time they came through.

"We're trying to establish a timeline. I need to know what was going on here from last night until the body was found this morning?"

"Do I look like a hall monitor?"

"No, but let's start with what you were doing. When was the last time you saw Mr. Douglas?"

Kevin thought for a moment while his watch beeped. "I guess I last saw him at dinner."

"You guess or it was?" Davis asked dryly.

"Yes, dinner," Kevin replied.

"Did anything unusual happen at dinner? Did Mr. Douglas seem upset?"

"Only the typical arguments at the dinner table. Gabby was drunk, as usual, and started everyone off."

"Gabby? Do you mean Abigail Douglas?" Davis queried.

"Yes, Randall's wife, Abigail. She gets easily annoyed and drinks way too much. She likes to rope us all in so she doesn't stand out like a lush when she starts drinking."

"Why was she annoyed?"

"She didn't want to leave Texas and come to New Jersey to begin with. When we arrived and she found out her husband was playing down in Atlantic City, she was pretty ticked off. She's used to five star hotels, not closed up houses."

"So, what happened at the dinner table?"

"Everyone was fighting and began screaming around the table. Randall dragged us all up here as if he wanted to sign papers tomorrow. We later come to find out, the will hasn't been read yet. I got annoyed because we don't even know if the property is free and clear to purchase. Why waste our time? Then Randall was mad at Dean for pushing the envelope. So was the guy who showed up earlier, too. Obviously, he wants a piece of the action."

Davis snapped his head in Kevin's direction. "What other guy?"

Kevin shrugged. "I don't know, some dude showed up and was yelling at the girl living here. Megan, I think."

"He was yelling about the house?"

"Look, I couldn't hear the whole thing but I was on my way up the stairs before dinner and I heard some of it from the hall. It caught my attention because he was saying that Randall and Dean had pissed off a good part of the town. Apparently, no one wants us to buy in this area. But then he goes on to say, if anything is being sold, he wants a piece of the action."

"Did you catch a name?"

"No, but ask Megan. That's who he was yelling at."

Davis was scribbling in his book. "When did this happen?"

"Before dinner. Then everyone was yelling at dinner. Then the cop dude broke it all up and sent us packing. That's the last time I saw Randall. Today I heard everyone in the house start talking when they saw the police on the beach and Gabby running around saying Randall was missing, so I'm assuming he was the body floating in the brine."

"Once again, we must get confirmation, but Mrs. Douglas identified his photo."

Kevin's watch chimed several more times as he sat at the desk. He looked down to check the messages. "I really have to respond to this. Apparently, the word is spreading that Randall is dead and people at work are going nuts."

Davis put his hand up. "Just a few more questions, please? Can you tell me about your business? What's the name of the company and what's the focus?"

"Douglas Development. I'm surprised you haven't heard of us, Chief."

Davis paused for a second. "I believe I've heard the name in the news but details escape me."

"Randall Douglas started the company a long time ago. Douglas Development is a real estate development company that buys and sells large tracts of land. Usually for commercial properties or large housing developments. Projects have to net us fifty million dollars or more. There's a lot at stake here."

"Is he the sole owner?" Davis asked, staring at Mr. Shaw for reaction.

"Of course not. I own some of the company and so does Gabby." Kevin Shaw abruptly stood up and straightened his clothing. "I'm sorry, Chief. Unless I'm under arrest, which I highly doubt as this is a drowning, I should move on with my affairs. You'll have to contact our attorneys to get any other information you need about the company. I'm sure you're competent enough to do some research on your own." Kevin picked up his cell phone and walked out of the library.

Chapter Thirty

Andrew Davenport sat at the highly-polished desk in his office, reading a deposition regarding another lawsuit against the town. Although he would never admit it, there were times when he was tired of being the mayor. He enjoyed the perks, the attention, the respect, all access and ultimate authority but the job was wearing on him. He had a golden parachute but it was nothing compared to the money he would make if he could buy the Stanford property. New zoning laws were being proposed which could be quite profitable for him, if he was positioned properly before they went through.

He'd planned to ask Rose to sell the land six months ago, but then when he realized she was dying, he thought he'd wait and talk to her son. Dean Stanford didn't want his mother's property. He was a playboy looking for some flash.

"Damn, Dean Stanford." Andrew tapped his pen on his blotter. He should have approached Rose immediately after the Hurricane. No one in the Stanford family knew about the proposed zoning change, so the land he needed didn't mean much to them but it meant the world to Andrew.

Even if the Stanford's held out for a greater sum, Andrew planned on cleaning up, but he never anticipated having to deal with Megan Stanford. He thought she was gone for good and then she unexpectedly showed up as if she owned the place.

The small war between the Stanfords and the Davenports had been growing for a while. Andrew looked at a photo of his son, Jeff, as he drummed his fingers on the desk. The kid was in jail, awaiting trial. Andrew reminded himself to call the high-priced lawyer he had hired to see if there was an appeal they could file to overturn his charge. Sometimes, when the discussion involved the right amount of palm grease, evidence could go missing and witnesses could forget things they saw. He would press the guy in the morning. Andrew was paying him enough to move mountains at this point.

Next, he had to figure out what was going on with Rose's estate. Megan said the will hadn't been read yet, but knowing Theodore Harrison Carter the way he did, Andrew was sure the will had been read, signed and filed as soon as possible after Rose's death. Andrew was convinced he knew exactly where Teddy would have filed the will for probate. Once filed, Andrew could access a copy of it by submitting a short legal form and paying the public records fee. It would make very interesting reading to find out who inherited the bulk of the estate although Dean Stanford sure acted as if Misty Manor and the town property was his to sell. He'd have to move fast to make sure no one else threw their hat in the ring, but he chuckled as he contemplated the wrinkle he had already thrown into their plans. No one would be able to use the land for the moment, he'd made sure of that.

Chapter Thirty-One

Davis walked out of the library, stopped in the hall and looked around the foyer. He noticed Abigail and Dean walking around the parlor with fresh drinks in hand. Kevin stomped upstairs as soon as he left the library to conduct unknown critical business.

Nick and Megan sat on the settee while Savannah paced back and forth across the cherry wood floor. Marie was mumbling and becoming anxious about starting dinner.

Davis cleared his throat and walked directly to the young woman. "Excuse me, is it Savannah?"

She looked up, fear registering in her eyes. "Me?"

Davis nodded his head. "Yes, are you Savannah Williams?"

Without answering, she nodded her head, eyes wide.

"Would you mind coming with me?"

At first, she didn't respond but then nodded her head once more while swallowing hard.

Davis gestured across the hall. "After you."

Savannah walked across the hall, into the library and waited for Chief Davis to direct her to the chair. He sat down beside her and pulled his pad out of his pocket.

"Your full name is Savannah Williams?"

"Yea," she said while watching the words he wrote on the pad.

"And you work for Douglas Development?"

"Yea."

Davis waited a moment for her to expand upon her answer but when she said nothing else he continued. "How long have you worked there?"

Savannah cocked her head and thought for a moment. "About eight years now."

Davis nodded in silence as he wrote. "And what is your job description there?"

"I'm the administrative assistant for Mr. Douglas. I type letters and make his appointments. I handle his contracts and do a lot of his paperwork."

"I see. Do you work for Mr. Shaw as well?"

Savannah nodded her head up and down. "I do, but Randall needs more paperwork done than Kevin."

Davis thought for a moment and then asked, "So, have you noticed any problems lately? Anything that would pose a problem in Mr. Douglas's life or business affairs?"

Savannah hesitated before speaking. "No, I don't think so."

"Really? Everything is hunky dory at work? No fights or delinquent bills?"

"Not that I know of," Savannah said as she shook her head.

"What time did you go to your room last night?"

"Excuse me?" Savannah said as her head snapped up in surprise.

"I'm sorry. I'm just trying to establish where everyone was last night until today," Davis explained.

"I went to bed after dinner. There was a bit of a disagreement and the policeman told all of us to go to our rooms."

"What time was that?"

Savannah shrugged. "I don't know, maybe 8pm?" Savannah watched as Chief Davis continued to write.

Chapter Thirty-Two

Nick sat up straight and stretched his neck side to side, causing his vertebrae to crack in relief. He rubbed the back of his neck and rolled his shoulders as he looked toward Megan.

"Do we have to sit here anymore?" She asked as she stood up and stretched her back.

"Probably not," Nick said. "Davis wanted me to watch and make sure your visitors didn't have an opportunity to compare notes before he got a chance to speak to them all."

"Do you think he's discovered anything important?"

"I have no idea," Nick whispered. "I can't talk about it, you know that. As a matter of fact, I probably can't stay here anymore as I would be too close to the case."

Megan snapped her head toward her boyfriend. "Wait, let me get this straight. You're telling me your chief has been in my library all day to make sure I don't have a murderer staying here as a guest and you can't stay?"

"That's right," Nick agreed.

Megan frowned as she continued. "So, because there may be a murderer, you have to leave?"

Nick slowly nodded his head up and down. He shrugged apologetically as he realized her intent. "Yea, I guess so."

"Fantastic way to offer protection," Megan scowled at his announcement. "That's fine, but make sure you take them all with you."

"Actually, Davis is probably going to tell them not to leave town for a while. He can't arrest anyone unless he has evidence or an admission, but he may caution them not to leave. He'll want them to stay until he gets the initial autopsy results at least."

A huge sigh escaped Megan's lips as she looked down and shook her head. "I can't believe this is happening again."

The pair turned their heads when they heard a noise in the hall. Davis was standing there looking at the two of them. "Miss Stanford, may I have a word with you?"

Megan felt her stomach knot as he called her name. Her reaction surprised her as she hadn't done anything wrong. Megan and Nick stood up and began to walk toward the hall. Davis held his hand up and motioned for Nick to back off.

"Not you, Nick. I would like to speak to Miss Stanford alone."

Nick stopped as fleeting expressions of surprise and anger flashed across his face.   "Okay, if that's what you want. We found the body together so I thought you'd want my take on things."

"I do," Davis said as he nodded his head, "and I'll get to your statement, later."

Nick nodded and turned back to the parlor as Davis called out to him.

"Nick, why don't you go to the station and help them with the reports. While you're there, you can write up your own statement. Then check with the medical examiner and see if he has any preliminary results." Davis turned back to Megan and gestured toward the library. "After you, please."

Megan headed toward the library but looked back at Nick over her right shoulder. Knowing how upset she was, he smiled and winked to offer her encouragement.

"Miss Stanford?"

Megan turned back toward Davis and followed him through the door and over to the chairs he had been using by the mahogany desk. "Please, take a seat."

Megan sat down in the chair in front of the desk and Davis choose the chair to her right. She looked around the formal library with a smile. Three days ago, she had sat on the other side of the same desk, signing papers to allow Teddy to start the process of settling Grandma Rose's estate. Now she sat in the chair feeling like she was summoned to the principal's office for unknown reasons.

Where was Teddy? She left three messages asking him to call her back. He didn't know about Mr. Douglas and she may need him if the interview she was about to have went wrong.

"Miss Stanford, can you please tell me what's been going on around here?" Davis asked as he settled himself into the chair, obviously expecting a long answer.

"I don't know," she said as she shrugged her shoulders.

"You were here when all these people arrived?"

"Yes sir, sort of," Megan said, nodding her head in confirmation.

"So, start from the beginning. When did they get here? What do they want?"

Megan's smile was rueful. "I'm convinced they want Misty Manor."

"So, tell me about it." Davis nodded his head to encourage her to talk.

"I don't know where to begin." Megan hesitated for a few seconds. "Last Friday, I was here completing paperwork with Teddy."

"Teddy who?" Davis asked as he took out his pad and pen. He clicked the top of the pen and prepared to take notes.

Megan looked at the pad while she spoke. "Theodore Harrison Carter. He's my grandmother's attorney."

"Oh, I get it, Teddy." Davis nodded his head. Theodore Harrison Carter had been a resident of Misty Point for many years. "Can you tell me what kind of paperwork?"

Megan shook her head side to side. "Not really, it was very complicated but it was to start the process of settling Rose's estate."

"Interesting. So, let's get right to the question on everyone's mind." Davis looked at her sideways. "Do you know who stands to inherit?"

"Not really," Megan said truthfully. "There are many parts to the will, according to Teddy. Grandma Rose had a lot of different holdings."

"Your father must think he's inheriting Misty Manor if he already brought a real estate developer to look at it. How big is the property? Do you know?"

Megan shrugged. "I'm not sure but I seem to remember it's somewhere in the ballpark of ten acres."

"Including the lighthouse?" Davis asked.

"Yes, and all of the beach. Grandma Rose owned the whole Point. As you know, she owned a bit of property in town as well."

Davis let out a slow long whistle. "We're talking a lot of money."

Megan frowned at Davis. "Is that really the most important thing you can think of right now?"

"Inheriting money makes people do crazy things," Davis said with a nod.

Megan paused. "I don't like where you're going with this. What are you implying?"

"I'm not implying anything, Miss Stanford. We don't know who inherited the bulk of the estate. Could be you, or your father or Teddy might have a personal stake in this."

Megan frowned. "What does all this have to do with Randall's death?"

"Nothing." Davis smiled to try to disarm her. "I'm simply collecting facts."

"Then please stick to the topic. I don't have to answer all your questions."

"No ma'am, you don't," Davis said, nodding his head in agreement. "Unless, of course, we find something unexpected on the autopsy."

"It seems to me you've already found something suspicious or you wouldn't be asking all these questions."

Davis simply shrugged his shoulders. "Can I ask a few more and then I promise I'll let you go."

Megan sighed. "Go ahead."

"Please tell me what happened after you signed the papers with Teddy."

Megan thought for a minute. "Well, it was raining very hard. As Teddy went to leave, there was a heavy banging on the door. It turned out to be my father and this man, Randall Douglas." Megan shook her head. "You would have thought they were college buddies the way they were laughing and carrying on."

"Really? That's interesting," Davis said. "What happened next?"

"Not much. After spending the morning upsetting people in town, my father acted as if they were checking into a hotel instead of his childhood home. They wanted rooms, expensive liquor, and a gourmet meal." Megan looked around and gestured with her hand. "Obviously, Misty Manor is in disrepair. From the moment I came back here, I was busy taking care of Grandma Rose until she died. My lousy father couldn't be bothered. He was too busy traipsing around Europe with his French girlfriend, Gigi."

Davis swallowed hard to avoid laughing at her description. He looked down at his pad while she continued.

"Misty Manor has eighteen bedrooms. Except for the few we've used, they haven't been cleaned in years. I told them they were welcome to remake their own beds and share the single can of tuna fish I had in the house."

"And what happened?"

"They took off to Atlantic City, which was fine by me."

Davis scribbled in his pad. "When did everyone else show up?"

"Saturday morning," Megan said, her voice becoming thick and her eyes moist. "Nick dragged me out for the first time since Grandma Rose died. As we drove home, I was starting to feel a bit more hopeful until we arrived at Misty Manor and the three of them were camped out on the front porch." Megan paused for a deep breath.

"Apparently, they couldn't get a room at a hotel so my father told them to come here. Thankfully, Marie agreed to come over and help me clean the house."

"Why bring them here?"

"I think he wanted some sort of opinion of New Jersey and the shore area. They were talking as if a sale was already worked out, but I don't know how someone can sell something they technically don't own yet."

Davis chewed on his inner cheek as he thought. "Do you think your father and Teddy could have some sort of agreement?"

Megan looked up. "I don't think so. If they do, Teddy is a great actor because he looked like he ate something nasty when he saw my father at the door."

"Stranger things have happened," Davis suggested. "I never do this, but I'm going to give you a bit of advice." Davis paused to make sure Megan wouldn't object. "I don't know how the will is going to read, but if you're part of it, I'd hire an independent forensic auditor to go over the books as soon as you can."

Megan was quiet as she digested his comment. She nodded and said, "Thank you. I'll keep that in mind. So, when can I expect all these people to leave?"

Davis shook his head. "I have no idea, Ms. Stanford. I'm sure Abigail Douglas will want to stay and make arrangements for her husband. I have to see what the preliminary exam from the medical examiner shows as well." Davis cleared his throat. "I have one more delicate question before we finish."

Megan's fatigue began to show on her face. "If you must, but please make this your last one."

Davis didn't seem to know how to phrase the question. "Your father indicated he wasn't around here last night because he had some sort of date? Do you know anything about that?"

"A what?" Megan sat up straight. "You have to be kidding me. He said that?"

"Well, he said he had some sort of private engagement last night. I was wondering who you think he might have been meeting." Davis looked sheepish as he asked the question.

Megan laughed, but anger seeped into her eyes and face. "I have no idea and I hope I don't find out because I'll get very upset."

"Thank you for answering my questions, Ms. Stanford." Davis placed his pad back in his pocket as he watched Megan stand up and stretch. When she started for the door, he followed her into the hall. For the first time that afternoon, the parlor was empty and the house was quiet.

"I don't know where everyone went," Megan said. "It certainly appears they've all disappeared."

Davis looked around and found no one waiting. "Thank you, Ms. Stanford. I'm sure I'll be in touch." Davis slapped his cap on his head and walked out the front door.

Chapter Thirty-Three

Megan stood in the hall for a moment, too drained to think. No one was around. She walked toward the kitchen, but Marie was nowhere to be found. Wandering back into the parlor, Megan picked up the glasses and plates which littered the room. She found wadded napkins on the floor and melted ice cubes on the table. She knew the house had been neglected for a long time, but there was no reason for grown adults to act like they were visiting a dump. Misty Manor was a beautiful Grand Victorian which would be restored to its former beauty someday.

Holding the glasses, she walked down the hall toward the kitchen when the phone began to ring. She set everything down and answered, "Hello?"

"Hi, is Megan Stanford there?" Megan's stomach knotted as she tried to figure out who would want to call her. She hoped it wasn't the press.

"This is she," Megan replied.

"Hi, this is Barbara Moss from Cape Shore Hospice. I'm calling to let you know I'm sorry for the loss of your grandmother."

"Thank you," Megan said, a bit confused.

"I'm the bereavement counselor from the hospice and I wanted to call to see how you were doing. Grief is a very individual emotion and there's no right or wrong way to feel, but I wanted you to know we were thinking about you."

Megan took a moment before she spoke. Considering what had just happened, she needed to stop herself from laughing and crying at the same time.

"To be honest, I haven't had time to work it through, yet," Megan said.

"I understand, it can take a while for things to settle down," Barbara said.

And you don't know the half of it, Megan muttered to herself.

"Excuse me?" Barbara asked.

"Oh, sorry. I was thinking about something. I'm sorry but I have to go now," Megan said.

"Oh, is it okay if we check on you again? Maybe I can stop by?"

"I don't know," Megan said. "Maybe."

Barbara paused for a moment. "How about if I call again next week? Then you can decide."

"That would be great," Megan said. "Ok, goodbye now."

"Goodbye and once again, so sorry for your loss."

Megan shook her head and hung up the phone. Three days ago, she was so depressed she barely left the house or ate. Today, she was back in the middle of a disaster.

Megan recollected the glasses she had set down to answer the phone and was about to walk to the kitchen when she heard a knock. She shifted the glasses to one hand so her other hand was free to cautiously open the front door.

"Meg, how are you?" Amber stood at the door next to Georgie. Eyes wide, she looked at Megan holding several glasses and paper waste.

Megan looked at her two friends and said, "Oh guys, I'm so glad you're here. You're certainly a sight for sore eyes."

Georgie nodded towards the beach. "You looked awful earlier. We wanted to check on you but we decided to wait until the police were all gone."

"Come in, please come in," Megan said as she stepped back from the door. Her friends entered the house and realizing Megan was cleaning, helped her straighten tables and chairs and carry all the dishes into the kitchen.

"Do you want me to start washing these for you?" Georgie asked as she placed them in the large sink.

"No, I can do them later. I'd rather get out of the house and be with you guys for a bit. I don't have the heart to go back to the beach so let's go out the back door."

"Great," Amber said. "I need to get more steps in today so let's go for a walk."

Georgie stood behind Amber and rolled her eyes. Megan started to giggle.

"What?" Amber asked, pretending to be incensed. "You should stuff yourself inside corporate clothing all week. Forget having a watch that transmits all your steps to your company benefits department, just so they can log millions of steps for their heart health program."

Megan and Georgie laughed at her frustration.

"Go ahead and laugh," Amber said as she pointed to Georgie. "You get to wear a bathing suit all day. When it gets windy you're allowed to put on sweats and you never have to worry about hair and makeup."

"In case you didn't notice, I have jeans on at the moment," Georgie said, pointing at her outfit of designer jeans, round neck summer blouse and running shoes.

Megan shook her head. "I guess I don't have to worry about hair and makeup, considering I don't have a job." She was quiet for a few moments. "Although, I'm going to have to do something soon."

Georgie looked at her friend. "Why? What's going on with Misty Manor?"

"I have no idea," Megan said. "I feel like I'm living in a circus."

The three women walked out the back door, crossed the porch and headed toward the woods at the back of the property. "Remember all the fun we had at the gazebo when we were in high school?"

"Oh, the stories we could tell," Amber said as she turned to them. "But don't ever tell a soul anything you've ever heard in the gazebo. I mean it."

Georgie smiled. "It'll cost you."

Amber made a face at Georgie as they crossed the expansive back lawn. She turned to Megan, "So do you know what's going to happen to the cottages back here?"

"No, I don't know anything yet," Megan said. "The construction crew took down the two cottages which were most damaged by Hurricane Sandy. Everything else was put on hold until the last police investigation was done. With everything else that happened and Grandma Rose dying, I didn't have the heart to start it all up again."

Georgie put an arm around her friend's shoulders and squeezed her close. "We're so sorry about your grandmother. She was a great lady."

"She sure was," Amber said. "We all loved her."

Megan felt several tears slide down her face as she nodded her acknowledgement.

Georgie punched her in the arm. "Race to the gazebo. The loser has to buy pizza." She then turned to Amber. "If you lose, you actually have to eat the pizza."

"Oh, no way that's happening." Amber took off and raced Georgie toward the gazebo, but Georgie's daily runs as a lifeguard allowed her to easily win without taking a deep breath. Amber arrived next while Megan walked behind and laughed at her two friends.

The gazebo was tucked back in the middle of the woods and had been somewhat of an escape for Rose. The base was made of marble which was brought back from Europe on one of John Stanford's trips as a sea captain in the early nineteen-hundreds. Six thin marble pillars rose from the base and were topped by a metal dome complete with decorative inlay. The structure had decorated this hidden garden spot for over a hundred years, but was now tarnished. The rose bushes, which had so beautifully decorated the surrounding area, died when the ocean washed over the beach during Hurricane Sandy and settled on the property behind the house.

The three women climbed inside the structure and sat on the marble floor. Georgie turned to Megan. "Honey, we don't want to look like we're prying information from you, but we're worried. We haven't been able to have a good talk since the funeral. Seriously, what's going on? Are you okay?"

Megan looked at her two dear friends. "I'm sorry. I know I slipped into a major pity party after Rose died." Megan shook her head. "It was all too much. Leaving my job in Detroit, coming back to New Jersey and the whole police thing." Megan paused for a moment. "I hadn't been back to see Grandma Rose and Misty Manor in seven years. So much neglect, I felt guilty I didn't check in on her as much as I should have."

"Stop, you can't beat yourself up about that," Georgie said. "No offense to your father, but he was her son. He could have done something."

"No offense taken, you guys know what a jerk he always was. That's the reason Grandma was so protective of me to begin with. I should have been more grateful."

"Megan, you were here for her when she needed you," Amber pointed out. Seeing the sad expression on her friend's face, Amber said, "Stop already. I hate to bring this up, but there's more chatter in town we need to talk about."

Megan looked at Georgie who nodded her head in agreement. "It's true. Apparently, your father and Mr. Douglas were vocal in their intent to buy up a lot of property. They mentioned they were going to turn Misty Manor and another part of town into an executive getaway."

Amber nodded. "Year round, no less."

"Now, the tongues are wagging about this guy dying. The word on the street is he was murdered." Georgie shifted position.

"I don't believe this," Megan said. "The police just left. Gossip spreads faster than lightening around here."

"You're surprised?"

"No, I guess not. Look, here's the deal. Teddy hasn't officially read the will to us yet. I saw him Friday and he said he was going to come back in a few business days to go over things. I've called him a couple of times. He answered me on Saturday when all these people showed up. I'm kind of embarrassed but with not working for a while, I needed money to buy food. I would have skipped some meals but they think they're guests of Randall Douglas."

"In terms of you not eating, that's exactly what we were worried about," Georgie said dryly.

"I wish these people would get out of Misty Manor as soon as possible," Megan said with a frown. "They're awfully rude and ungracious and have only caused trouble since arriving here. Unfortunately, they're going to have to stay until the police investigation is over. Then his wife can make arrangements to have the casket sent back to Texas."

"Do you think he was murdered?" Georgie asked.

"I'm not sure. I thought I was helping a stranded dolphin. I went to clear seaweed away and was shocked to find a human eye staring back at me." Megan turned to Georgie. "You were there and I'm sure you heard more of what they found than I did. What do you think?"

"I'm not exactly sure what they found," Georgie admitted. "They had him out of the water by the time I got there. Something must have looked wrong because that wasn't a typical extraction."

Megan thought for a moment, trying to bring back awful memories of the scene on the beach. "I can't wait around this time. I should help the police figure out what happened. The sooner we figure this out, the sooner they'll all be out of here."

Georgie looked at Amber and shrugged. She then reached out and placed her hand on Megan's arm. "We'll help you out as much as we can."

"You will?" Megan asked with a smile.

"Yes, but promise us you won't do anything dumb this time."

"Dumb?"

"Yes, that means you don't go anywhere or do anything dangerous without telling us first."

"It's a deal," Megan said as she extended her hand to her friends. "Just like the old days."

Chapter Thirty-Four

Nick looked up when Davis entered the police station. The Chief walked into his small office, circled to the back of his desk and threw down his hat as he dropped into his aged office chair. Davis leaned back, propped his feet on the desk and closed his eyes.

Getting back to his statement, Nick reread what he had written and saved the document. He planned to read it once more, then save it to his digital report file. He would print a copy for Davis as well. Silently, he reviewed the information. He started from his arrival at Misty Manor the night before. He recorded facts involving the drunken behavior at dinner and continued through finding the body during his walk on the beach with Megan.

After saving his document, Nick peered through the window Davis had in his office and watched him sit up in his chair and begin to sort through the pile of messages on his desk. The Misty Point police station was old and overcrowded with furniture and file cabinets and there had been some minor damage from Hurricane Sandy. The water had risen to the base of the front door and a few feet inside, some from the initial tidal surge and the rest from the floodwaters which followed. Two of the file cabinets near the front door had rusted on the bottom and occasionally there was a waft of mildew odor when the heat was not turned up high enough, but the precinct made do with what they had.

Davis felt eyes on him and turned in Nick's direction. Catching Nick's stare, he jerked his head to the side to beckon him into the office.

"What's the status?" Davis asked as he sat back in his chair.

"I called the ME's office. They haven't officially done the post, but they're leaning in the direction of homicide." Nick picked up a pile of papers from the closest chair and put them on the corner of Davis's desk.

"State Police in there yet?" Davis asked as he watched Nick clear the seat and sit down.

"About an hour ago."

"What's your take on all this?"

Nick thought for a moment. "It's messed up as far as I'm concerned. Megan has been very upset since her grandmother died. I know you're not happy with the Stanford's, but she's not like her father. Megan is more like Rose was. She's going through a lot right now. She's grieving for her grandmother and feeling guilty she left New Jersey and took that job in Detroit, but she's a good person. Her father on the other hand? He's a class A jerk."

Davis frowned as he thought about the day. "Assuming this is a homicide, who do we have at the top of the list as the perp?"

Nick shook his head. "I don't know. This Douglas fellow shows up with Dean Stanford and apparently, they were obnoxious around town on Friday, drumming up plenty of gossip. The Stanfords own more than half the town. They trusted Rose would put the land into capable hands when she passed, but knew Dean would sell them out in a heartbeat. Anyway, we got Douglas, his wife, his partner and the assistant. None of them looked very happy to be there. It could be any one of them."

"But what would be the motive? I doubt it's bad travel arrangements," Davis observed.

"I know," Nick agreed.

"What about Stanford?" Davis asked while he cleaned his fingernails.

"I hope you mean Dean."

Davis nodded. "Let's go with that."

"I have no idea what business was going on between Dean and Randall Douglas, but I wouldn't be surprised by any accusation against him."

Davis nodded as he continued looking at his hands.

Nick looked up at Davis and gave him a quick flick of the head. "You've been here a long time. What do you think of the attorney?"

Davis pursed his lips together and considered the question. "Teddy?"

"Yeah, do you know him well? Is he to be trusted?"

"Just out of curiosity, why do you ask?"

"Apparently, he had Megan sign papers on Friday and then he disappeared. He told her she had some inheritance money coming her way, but she was too upset to read all the paperwork. She's not stupid and she assumed she could trust him without reading the fine details. Next thing we know Dean and Douglas show up and he disappears."

"For the record, I told her to get an independent auditor. But what's the point?"

"It's no secret Dean is an ass and Douglas is a well-known developer. The partner, Kevin Shaw, was already sizing up what kind of potential Misty Manor had if they turned it into a luxury retreat. Do you think Teddy could be some sort of silent partner? What if he let the two buffoons do the dirty work, but he's already making arrangements with all the money."

Davis thought for a moment. "I don't know, Nick. I've known Theodore Harrison Carter for a while. He's an eccentric kind of guy but he always seemed genuine. Rose was a generous woman and wanted to help everyone out. He always supported her decisions and made it happen. He didn't talk her out of things the way I've seen other lawyers do it."

Nick shrugged. "I don't know the guy, that's why I'm asking."

"But, I don't know what kind of fees he gets or whether he helps himself to the cookie jar," Davis acknowledged. "You better start looking for him. I'm sure he's part of the puzzle."

"You got it," Nick said.

"We have to do a background check on the rest of the group," Davis said. "Let's check out Douglas Development and see if we can pick up anything suspicious. When did the ME say he'll be done with the autopsy?"

"I think they're waiting for someone from the State," Nick said. "He'll call as soon as he's done to give us a preliminary finding."

Davis pointed his fingertips and placed them together.

"There's one more thing," Nick said.

"What's that?"

"Andrew Davenport showed up at Misty Manor yesterday. He was there to make a deal with Megan and Dean, except he wasn't sure who he should be talking to. Apparently, he's had his mind set on buying some of Rose's property. When he found out Randall was upping the ante, he got rather agitated."

"Now that's interesting," Davis said as he nodded his head. "I believe I heard something about that today."

"I don't know if Davenport was bothered enough to kill Randall," Nick said. "But Megan said he was hot under the collar about the property. We both know there's bad blood between the Davenports and the Stanfords."

"Enough to kill an innocent man?"

"Money makes people do strange things," Nick said as he shrugged his shoulders.

"Then go out and find me some evidence," Davis said as he pointed to the door.

"You got it, boss."

Chapter Thirty-Five

Megan stared at her phone as she wrestled with the decision to make the call. Four months prior, she'd been unceremoniously fired from the Detroit Virtual News, DVN for short, for digging up a little too much dirt, tying the newspaper's owner to a scandal. Her big reward turned out to be a pink slip. When she left, she told Marge, the newspaper's office mom, she would be in touch and let her know where she landed. After being out of Detroit for a month, Megan called her ex-landlady and released her apartment but she never called Marge.   Now she felt a twinge of guilt calling the office to get information. *Make the call.* Megan had no choice, she was desperate.

Megan pulled out her cell phone and scrolled through her contacts list tapping the screen when her thumb landed on Marge's name. She waited as the phone dialed and was eventually rewarded with a human voice.

"Detroit Virtual News, Marge speaking."

"Hi, Marge," Megan said softly.

"Oh my, how are you dear?"

"I'm ok, coming along."

"Are you still in New Jersey?" Marge asked.

Megan chuckled softly. "Yes, I am. How did you know?"

"I saw the obituary for your grandmother. Megan, it made national news."

"She was a very special woman."

"I knew you'd be there for the funeral," Marge said. "Your grandmother was precious to you."

Megan fell silent for a moment.

"Hello? Are you still there?"

"Yes, Marge. I was just thinking of Rose for a moment. It's still pretty unbelievable."

"I'm sorry if I upset you, dear. How are you? Are you okay?"

"Yeah, I'm as well as I could be," Megan said. "How's Ed?"

"Grumbling as usual. He misses you."

Megan laughed. "Hardly, he dumped me."

"He had to," Marge said. "He wanted to get away with a slap on the wrist. He pleaded with them for an hour, but no go."

"Well, I'm glad he tried," Megan said as she grimaced.

"Of course, he did," Marge protested. "He had no choice. Either follow directions or get out. He didn't speak for the entire day after you left."

"Not one peep?"

"Not one," Marge reaffirmed. "I've known him a long time. He felt bad. It ate him up."

"He never reached out to see how I was doing."

"Honey, he was afraid. So, what's going on? When are you coming back to Detroit?"

Megan shifted position. "Not for a while, Marge."

"Oh? So, you're staying in New Jersey?"

Megan could hear disappointment in her voice.

"Yes, for a while. I need to straighten out Grandma Rose's affairs before I do anything," Megan said.

"Hmm," Marge began. "And you thought you'd call and shoot the breeze?"

Megan smiled to herself. She could envision Marge standing in the office, hand resting on her plump hip.

"I could never get anything by you," Megan laughed.

"And I know you've tried," Marge said in her most officious voice which made Megan laugh harder.

"Guilty as charged."

"So, out with it then. What's up?"

Megan paused for a second before she began. "I need to do a little research on something and I don't have access to the same resources I did when I worked for Detroit Virtual."

"You're spying on someone?"

"C'mon Marge, I wouldn't call it that. It's just, ah, research."

"I see, and who or what exactly did you want to check out?"

"Well," Megan said, "I was looking for information on a company called Douglas Development from Texas. Also, the owner. A man named Randall Douglas."

"Anything illegal I should know about?"

"No, not at all," Megan said, arguing with herself that it wasn't illegal to check facts. There was a line that could be crossed between good investigative journalism and prying, but public fact checking was not off limits. "As a matter of fact, you soon may be able to use any information you find in relation to a breaking story."

"You're being very cryptic. Any chance you're going to tell me what's really going on?"

"Not now," Megan said in her sweetest voice.

"Hmm," Marge said. "This is interesting. I was hoping you'd get your former job back at DVN. But you may be more useful if you work in the field as a confidential informant."

"Me? A CI? You'd better ask Ed about that," Megan said with a shrug. "Besides, what value do you think I'd be in New Jersey?"

"Are you kidding me? There's a lot of interesting news coming out of the Garden State and most news is national now anyway."

"I don't know," Megan hesitated.

"Think about it," Marge encouraged. "You could be one of our very valuable sources. It might be a wonderful way to get back at DVN for firing you the way they did."

"I'll see," Megan said. "In the meantime, could you check on some info for me?"

Marge took a second to answer. "I'll do it and call you back as soon as I can, but in the meantime, think about what I asked you. I'm really sorry about your grandmother and I know you need time to grieve, but working may be an effective way to distract yourself."

"I appreciate it, Marge."

"You know I wouldn't do this if I didn't love you, right?"

Megan smiled. "I know. You're the best. That's why I don't want you, or me, for that matter, to get into any more trouble."

"I'll be discreet," Marge said. "Ok, let me go. I'll call you when I've got something, hopefully tomorrow."

"Thanks, Marge, and send my love to Ed."

"Will do, honey. Get a good night's sleep and believe me, I'll be in touch."

Chapter Thirty-Six

Pain slashed through her head as Abigail Douglas rolled to her side and opened one eye. She waited until the throbbing subsided before she moved again. Dry mouth, nausea and dizziness flooded in next. Normally she could hold her liquor better than this, but yesterday was too much to handle.

It took a moment for details to come back to her. Was it a dream or did it really happen? Was Randall dead? This wasn't the first time she hosted a severe hangover as a result of his behavior. Gambling, drinking, infidelity, control, anger, but always the life of the party. After thirty years of dealing with him, she'd had enough.

Abigail could have divorced him ten times over and there were times when Randall had made her generous offers to do so, but she wasn't letting the bastard off the hook that easy. He was worth much more as a husband than an ex. With the divorce, she would have been given a decent settlement but it would have dried up and she'd never be able to exact revenge. He had enough lawyers and influential colleagues to be forever shielded from any other recourse.

They met and fell in love in college. They had no money, no support and Randall almost didn't make it to graduation. Abigail was his classmate and had caught his eye many times. She was beautiful back then and smart. She agreed to help him with his studies and they quickly became good friends.

Randall was smart, street smart. He would network, listen, and had a silver tongue. He knew how to broker a deal and always to his advantage. Who knew he'd become filthy rich? If they stayed married, half of whatever Randall had was hers.

Abigail finally rolled onto her back. Her head continued to swim. She knew she should be doing something today, but couldn't focus. Call the police? Arrange a funeral? How the hell does one go about transporting a body? She was dizzy. Maybe start with a strong cup of coffee, then she could make a list. Abigail knew she had to contact someone on the board of directors of Douglas Development unless Kevin had already done so. She hadn't thought to speak to Kevin yesterday. They both owned large parts of the company, but her share was larger if her memory served correctly. Abigail suddenly realized she had a lot to do, thanks to another mess involving Randall. The sad part was deep down, somewhere tucked far away, a piece of her heart still loved the man she married.

Chapter Thirty-Seven

Marie filled the coffee pot and placed it on the warmer. Next to it, she placed cups, cream, and a crystal bowl filled with sugar. She imagined after yesterday's events, the group would need several gallons of rich, hot coffee to become functional today. Opening the refrigerator, she pulled out a dozen eggs, shaved cheese, bacon and sausage. Randall's death had softened her a bit toward the house guests, prompting her to make a hearty breakfast for those who wanted a home cooked meal.

Marie's hands shook and she felt a dull aching in her chest as she thought about Randall Douglas. She had only known the man a day or two, but the suddenness and circumstances of his death was a bit hard to grasp. It didn't help to have the chief of police hanging around asking questions all day either.

"Hello, beautiful."

Marie jumped when she felt an arm slip around her waist. Two eggs dropped out of her hands and smashed on the floor. "Oh, Dean," she said as she placed the rest of the eggs on the counter. "You scared me."

"Sorry, didn't mean to do that," Dean Stanford said as he leaned around Marie to grab a cup. "I was trying to get a cup of coffee, but it's also the first time we've been alone since I came back to Misty Manor."

"It's been a long time since we've talked to each other period," Marie said dryly.

"I know and I've been meaning to make up for that. Is the coffee ready?" Dean offered a large smile as he pressed against Marie's shoulder.

"The coffee is ready, but breakfast will be a little longer." Marie quickly stepped away. Turning, she picked up a roll of paper towels and squatted to clean the mess on the floor. With broad strokes, she gathered the shells and raw egg toward her.

"I can wait forever, darlin, if I have to," Dean said, slyly.

Marie stopped in front and looked him square in the face. "You have to be kidding me. I haven't heard from you in weeks. I helped Megan take care of your mother while she was dying. It's bad enough you didn't have the decency to come home and pay your respects to your mother, now you're acting like nothing happened around here yesterday."

Dean stepped back and held his hands up. The coffee cup tilted as his finger slipped around the handle. Trying to right the cup, hot coffee spilled onto his hand and he quickly banged the cup on the counter.

"Hey, back off," Dean said as he whirled on Marie. "Randall was a good guy, but he's gone now. If anyone loses on that deal, it'll be me. I was trying to let you know how much I missed you."

Marie couldn't contain her laughter as it rose from her chest. "That's rich. Are you missing Gigi the same way?"

"Gigi?" Dean appeared shocked. "She was nothing to me, Marie. You know that."

"Really? That's interesting because every time Megan tried to reach you about your mom, all we heard was you were busy or at some affair with Gigi."

"Hey, you know you have to do a bit of networking when you're trying to close a deal."

Marie frowned. "Oh, and how did that deal work out for you, Dean?"

Dean shrugged and leaned forward to add cream and three sugars to his coffee.

"I don't usually consider myself stupid," Marie went on as she shook her head. "Megan tried to reach you so many times. I can't imagine how she would feel if she knew we were talking on the phone as often as we were, that you were asking me to feed you information. I feel so guilty now that I realize your only concern was with your mother's estate and not her welfare."

"That's a very nice speech, Marie, but I don't really need a scolding right now. My mother passed away a few weeks ago."

Marie's face turned red with anger as she contemplated throwing a cup of hot coffee in his face. A sudden creak of the floor had them both turned toward the door in time to watch Abigail walk into the room, appearing worse than expected after last night.

"Abigail, how are you this morning?" Dean asked as he attempted to look concerned.

Abigail looked back and forth between Dean and Marie before she walked toward the coffee pot. "I'm sorry if I'm interrupting something. I need some hot coffee and two aspirin right now."

Dean immediately put down his cup to pick one up for Abigail. As Marie headed back to the stove, she raged as she heard his smooth voice. "Let me help you with that. What an awful day we had yesterday, losing someone we both loved so much. You must have a million things to do, planning for your husband's funeral in addition to becoming the new owner of Douglas Development."

Chapter Thirty-Eight

An hour later, Marie was placing steaming dishes of hot scrambled eggs, bacon, sausage and toast with butter on the side bar. She added some pastries, thinking the sugar may help those with a hangover. Waiting around the parlor the day before, she lost track of each guest as they were called in to speak to Chief Davis. A lot of the liquor disappeared but other than Dean and Abigail, she had no idea who had been inebriated and who had not.

Megan walked into the dining room and looked at Marie. She noted the strained face, the tense posture and gave her a questioning glance. She continued to pan around the room until her eyes rested on Dean and Abigail sitting at the table. Dean took a long gulp of coffee as Abigail sipped at hers half-heartedly and leaned her head on her hand. Within minutes, Kevin and Savannah walked into the dining room. Tentatively, they looked around and approached Abigail before serving themselves.

Kevin placed an arm around the back of Abigail's shoulders. As she turned toward him, he leaned down to plant a kiss on her forehead. "Abigail, I am so sorry for your loss. You must be beside yourself right now."

Savannah came up behind them and placed her hand on Abigail's other shoulder. With barely a whisper, she said, "I'm so sorry, Mrs. Douglas."

Abigail stood, and turned toward the pair to pull them into a small group hug. "When Randall called us here, I had no idea we would wind up in a mess like this. I still can't believe he's gone."

Megan stood on the side, uncomfortable with what to do and how to share her condolences with the recent widow. With a final squeeze, Abigail released her friends. Megan took the opportunity to approach her and offer her thoughts as well.

The rest of the group filled coffee cups, plates and sat around the dining room table. Dean refreshed his coffee and sat down as well.

Marie stood near the sideboard, alternately freshening the food and wiping her hands on a dish towel.

The room was quiet at first. Utensils scraped along plates as the sound of spoons glided against coffee cups.

Abigail took a sip of coffee then slammed her cup on the table. "This is ridiculous. Stop acting like we're in a funeral parlor. Please, have a conversation. Talk about anything so I can hear words or noise or something."

The table guests looked at each other sideways, sipping coffee and apprehensively clearing their throats. Finally, Abigail looked at Megan. "Do you mind if I ask a question?"

Megan swallowed her coffee. "Of course not. I hope I can answer."

"Why were we all questioned like criminals yesterday? Why aren't we allowed to leave the state until we get permission from Chief Davis?"

Megan looked up and noticed the entire group waiting for her answer. "I, I don't know exactly."

Kevin tilted his head and frowned. "Your boyfriend is a cop in this town. I'm sure he must have given you the inside scoop."

"No, he didn't. As a matter of fact, the reason he left is because he didn't want any confusion."

"Well, then why do you think we all were questioned?"

Megan put her coffee mug down on the table and looked at Marie who turned and busied herself stacking the empty plates from the sideboard. Dean looked down at the table to hide the smirk on his face.

"I don't have any specific details. If there are any, they weren't shared with me. I can tell you there are specific laws surrounding an unexpected death in this state. I assume the police were following a protocol of sorts."

"What kind of protocol?" Abigail asked.

"I don't know," Megan shrugged. "When someone dies, the police have to be called to check things. They have a duty to make sure a crime wasn't committed."

"You were the one who found him," Kevin said. "Did it look like a crime scene?"

Megan's face reddened. "I don't know." Her voice dropped to a whisper. "At first, I thought it was a dolphin or something caught in seaweed. I was shocked when I realized it was Randall." Megan's hands started shaking. "I screamed and Nick ran over. He sent me out of the water and called it in to the police station."

"Well, what did he look like?" Kevin asked. Abigail's head whipped around toward him while Savannah gasped at his insensitivity.

Megan's mouth worked for a moment while she tried to find words. "I couldn't see much through the seaweed. I remember seeing his eye. His eye was open."

Abigail began crying. "Does that mean anything?"

Megan took a deep breath before she answered. "I don't know. It was apparent he had died hours before. His skin was blue." Megan shook her head side to side. "Are you sure you want to talk about this?"

Abigail looked at her through red eyes. "Not really, but I need to know what happened to Randall."

"Ok," Megan nodded. "Like I said, when someone dies unexpectedly, the police or the medical examiner need to examine the scene to determine if there was any foul play. Maybe they saw something out of the ordinary and need to be sure."

"I can understand that," Abigail said as she played with her napkin.

Seeing an opportunity for information, Megan asked, "Did Randall like the ocean? Does it seem normal he would be down by the jetty at night?"

"Not that I'm aware of," Abigail said. "He enjoyed seeing the ocean but he wasn't a man who looked forward to swimming or relaxing on the beach."

"Do you think he had too much to drink that night?" Megan asked.

"Maybe you should ask your father. He was pouring," Abigail frowned at Dean.

"Who me?" Dean asked. "I may have poured him a scotch or two, but he didn't seem drunk the last time I saw him."

"Seemed to me you were trying to loosen him up a bit," Kevin said. "Perhaps push him to make a sale."

Dean turned toward Kevin. "Forgive me for saying, but I wasn't the one who ordered any liquor to be delivered here in the first place."

Abigail let out a sob. "I didn't want anyone to get hurt. I just thought a drink or two would loosen everyone up. There was so much anger from the minute we arrived at the house. Randall called us here, but he never had the chance to tell us what he was thinking."

"Let's just say, there were a few people from town who weren't happy with what they were hearing from Randall and my father," Megan said as she threw an accusatory look over at Dean.

"We did nothing wrong. Randall was scoping out the town. Sure, we talked about doing a bit of business." Dean shrugged. "Some of the town folk may have overhead our conversation, but nothing had been decided yet."

Megan struggled to contain her anger. "What did you expect? Grandma Rose just died and you're stomping around town talking about rebuilding. Of course, people are going to be upset."

Savannah timidly asked, "Was there anyone upset enough to want to hurt Mr. Douglas?"

Kevin broke in. "That man who came here and yelled at Megan didn't seem very happy."

It took Megan a moment to realize Kevin was talking about the mayor, Andrew Davenport. "He's greedy, but I don't think he planned on killing anyone."

"Stop it," Marie said as she grabbed a napkin. The group looked up at her in surprise. She dabbed at her eyes as she said, "We don't know for sure Mr. Douglas was murdered. Please stop."

The group awkwardly fell silent.

Megan was the first to speak. "Marie's right. We don't know anything for sure and this conversation is insensitive to Abigail. How about I give Nick a call and see if he has anything to tell us. We can follow up from there. Is that okay?"

The group mumbled as they got up and left the room. From across the table, Abigail looked at Megan, a faint look of gratitude in her eyes.

Chapter Thirty-Nine

Megan stood up from the table and walked over to comfort Marie. She gave her a quick hug around the shoulders before turning toward Abigail. Her intention was to swallow her resentment toward the group and offer support but Abigail had already left the room.

"I'm not sure if she's upset," Marie said as she began to pick up dishes. "Yesterday, she didn't seem to care about anything except her next drink. Today, she's the weeping widow." Marie shook her head side to side as she continued to clear the dishes.

"What do you mean?" Megan asked as she helped to gather dishes.

"It's just a feeling," Marie said. "Everyone in the little entourage has been cranky and upset since they arrived. Abigail barely noticed her husband when he returned from Atlantic City with your father. Now, he's dead, and she's a proper grieving widow."

Megan followed Marie into the kitchen, scraped the dishes and placed them in the sink. "Marie, did Chief Davis talk to you yesterday?"

"No, he didn't. I kept hanging around, waiting for my turn in the hot seat, but he left without asking me."

"Well, he didn't expect to get an admission from each person he spoke to and I have a feeling you didn't hurt Randall."

"Of course, I didn't."

"If it turns out Randall Douglas was murdered, Chief Davis was hoping there may have been a witness to something which could lead them to the killer. Or maybe, someone could corroborate that Randall was drunk as a skunk and decided to go swimming in the middle of the night."

Without comment, Marie turned and began to rinse the dishes.

Megan leaned forward to see her face. "Marie? Is there something you want to tell me? Did you see something?"

Marie hung her head and shook it side to side.

Megan leaned back against the counter next to the sink, crossed her arms and stared at Marie. "I have a feeling you're not being honest."

Her face strained, Marie looked up at Megan. She struggled to find the proper words to express her thoughts, but before she could start, the kitchen telephone began to ring.

Marie glanced at the phone, then turned back to the sink. "You'd better get that, it may be important."

Megan scowled and answered the phone. "Hello?"

"Hey girlfriend, what are you doing?"

"Georgie? I'm not doing anything. I just got up and had a pretty awful breakfast."

"Really? Who did the cooking?"

"It wasn't the food. It was the company."

"Care to elaborate?" Georgie asked, trying to coax the rest of the story from her.

"Everyone was sitting around the breakfast table, pointing fingers as to who contributed to Randall Douglas's death."

"Oh, I see. Well go get changed because you're going for a run this morning."

"What kind of run?" Megan asked.

"The kind where you put your running shoes on and burn a few calories."

"Georgie, I don't think it's an appropriate time to start running again. I really need to make a few calls." Megan turned to see Marie turn off the water, dry her hands on a towel and leave the kitchen.

"It's the perfect time. I've been talking to some people by the beach and I need to show you something. The exercise will be good for you, too. Increased blood flow to the brain will help you think better."

Realizing her chance to talk to Marie had passed, Megan sighed and gripped the phone. "Okay, how are we doing this?"

"I'm running down to get you. We'll run back along the boardwalk together. I'm leaving now. Considering it's about a mile, I should be there in six minutes or so."

"Georgie, I have to change. Wait a few minutes before you start."

"Ok, I'll give you an extra ten minutes. Go dig out your running shoes."

Chapter Forty

Nick parked his car and walked into the police station. He entered the pit, walked behind his desk and placed his extra-large coffee and a bagel sandwich on the ripped blotter. He slid his chair back, took a seat and grabbed a stack of paperwork which sat to the right side of the desk. He needed to review his report, sign and submit it to the case file.

Ten minutes, a few bites of breakfast and half a cup of coffee later, Nick looked up to see Chief Davis striding into the pit. Davis gestured toward Nick and directed him into his private office. "Now."

Nick stood up and made his way over. Davis was standing near the fax in the corner waiting for something to print. He turned toward Nick and held up a large white envelope. "I received this report from the ME this morning. He's going to rule the developer's death a homicide. I'm waiting on one last result."

"What's he basing that on?" Nick asked as he watched the Chief pull a document from the machine.

Walking to his chair, the Chief smiled and held up the paper. "Apparently, our visitor didn't drown. According to the report, there was no water in his lungs upon autopsy. As he was fully dressed, we can only assume he wasn't planning to swim."

"We know it wasn't a dry drowning," Nick said.

"No, there was a large gash on his head, but it wasn't typical for falling on rocks, assuming he was on the jetty." Reading the report, Davis continued. "They found green glass in the wound, typical of a wine bottle."

"Are you telling me someone hit him upside the head?" Nick asked.

"Looks that way," Davis said. "In addition to that, we got a report from the lighthouse keeper, Billy. He said he saw two people on the jetty the night before Randall Douglas was found. Douglas wasn't out there alone."

"Did he have any more details? Man, woman, tall, short?"

"No, it was dark, so no additional details." Davis finished reading the paragraph on the fax and tossed it on the desk. "It says here that, Douglas had a touch of heart disease and cirrhosis as well. Seems he liked his steak and drink."

"Someone didn't like him," Nick said as read the write up on the head wound.

"Okay, let's talk this out," Davis looked over toward Nick. "There's a lot of people in that house right now. It may not necessarily be one of them, but you've spent more time with them than I have. What's your take?"

Nick thought it over. "Let's look at his partner, Kevin Shaw. Maybe he gets to inherit the business now that Douglas is gone. Maybe the wife has a stake in the business as well. None of them were particularly happy to be in New Jersey."

"So, we check out the business," Davis said. "What about the secretary?"

Nick made a face. "She's an administrative assistant. She did all of Douglas's paper work, but what would she have to gain?"

Davis nodded his head in agreement. "Okay, next? Hey, while you're over there, start adding their names to the white board."

Nick stood up, grabbed a blue marker and started adding names to the board. "We know Dean Stanford is an ass and wanted to close the sale on Misty Manor to make a quick buck. But, even if the guy pulled out, that wouldn't necessarily be a reason to kill him."

"Unless Dean was just pissed off, drunk and making stupid decisions."

"True, he is a reactive jerk," Nick said, continuing to write on the board. "Especially when he drinks."

"Okay, next?" Davis studied the board.

"Random stranger?" Nick suggested.

"How does that play out?"

"Randall is annoyed I broke up the party and goes down to the beach to continue drinking. He trudges to the water with a wine bottle. We know there's some gang activity during the summer. Maybe someone tries to mug him. He resists. They grab the bottle and hit him over the head."

"It's a possibility," Davis said, "but not likely. Who else is in the mix?"

Nick looked up at his boss. "I don't know what Andrew Davenport was up to but from what we heard, he was pretty hot under the collar about a possible sale. He was at Misty Manor screaming at Megan. She wasn't even involved in their business."

"Maybe he was protecting the interest of the town," Davis suggested.

Nick made a face. "You really believe that?"

Davis waited a few seconds before he smirked. "No, the guy is an ass, like his kid."

"Who will hopefully rot in jail," Nick added.

"But I have no idea what his personal interest would be, so we'll have to consider that."

"I can't believe he'd show his face after what Jeff did to Megan," Nick said, visibly angry and clenching his fist.

Davis was silent for a few seconds, but then started to speak. "So that brings up your girlfriend. Sorry, but have to ask the question. Would she benefit if this guy was dead?"

Nick bristled as he looked at his chief. "Come on Davis, lay off. First, she vomited from shock when we found the body. She's been beside herself ever since these people showed up and she's angry because she knows Rose wouldn't want any of this."

"That's my point. This guy dies, and Douglas Development goes away," Davis argued.

"Dean Stanford would find another developer." Nick said with a gesture. "The one thing Megan kept saying is that the will hasn't been read yet. The attorney had her sign some papers, went to file them and hasn't been seen since. Megan's not sure of the legalities of anything or whether the property is even clear to be sold."

"If Dean duped them and then couldn't provide the property, I could see Douglas getting real upset."

"That would make sense if Dean Stanford was the one with the head injury." Nick agreed as he looked back at the Chief. "And then there's the attorney."

"Teddy?"

"Yeah. Any new thoughts?"

Davis rubbed his chin. "Theodore Harrison Carter. Quirky kind of guy. He made all the arrangements when Rose decided to donate to the hospital or nursing home. Same thing with the local library and police station. She owned most of this town and the Point but was always a generous woman and a good soul. Teddy's had a good career. He had nothing to gain from her death or Randall's for that matter."

"I don't know him," Nick said.

"He's old blood in this town," Davis said. "I have no idea how much Rose paid him or what their arrangements were, but he wouldn't have needed to steal from her. She would have given him anything he asked."

"I agree," Nick said. "But, he's nowhere to be found. Do you have a direct number?"

"I'll handle finding Teddy," Davis said, looking at the white board. "Any other immediate suspects?"

"No one other than Marie was at the house," Nick said.

Davis reviewed the entire whiteboard. "Okay, we have to do some digging. I'll get in touch with Teddy and have a detective start looking into Douglas Development. I want to know the life insurance beneficiary for Randall Douglas." Davis turned to Nick. "You go out there and tell them the report isn't ready yet. Make sure no one leaves town for now and tell them Randall's body hasn't been released yet."

"I'm on it," Nick said as he put the marker down.

"One of these folks is a killer. Let's get the bastard."

Chapter Forty-One

Megan dug out her running shoes and the only clothes she could find suitable enough for a run. While in high school, she used to run with Georgie when she trained for lifeguard tournaments. Megan tried to keep up with running in college to circumvent the freshman fifteen, but once she started working as a reporter for Detroit Virtual News, her free time had quickly vanished. Moving back to New Jersey and having such proximity to the beach and boardwalk, she was inspired to start exercising again and on a few occasions, she found herself considering an early morning walk, but the timing was impossible with Grandma Rose being ill. Then, once Rose passed, her inspiration and desire were gone.

Pulling her hair into a pony tail, Megan laced up her shoes and went downstairs to wait for Georgie. She opened the front door to enjoy the ocean view while she waited and was surprised to see Georgie on the porch, her foot propped up on the railing while she stretched. "I didn't know you were here."

"I got here a few minutes ago," Georgie said as she reached out for her foot. "I opened the door and gave a small shout, but no one answered so I decided to wait out here."

"Oh, sorry about that," Megan said as she watched her friend pull the bottom of her running shoe to her backside in a vigorous stretch. "Listen, I haven't been running in a long time. I may need to stop in the first half-mile."

"You'll do fine. We can slow down if we have to," Georgie said, pulling her leg off the railing. "Let's go."

The pair walked down off the porch and made their way across the lawn and sand to the beginning of the boardwalk. The day was warm, the breeze smelled great and the water almost looked blue-green in certain areas. "Okay, we'll start with a slow pace and pick it up once we warm up."

"If I can breathe," Megan said, feeling her body tighten more so from anxiety than being out of shape.

"Try not to think about it," Georgie said as she took off in a light job. "Just relax and enjoy the exercise. What's going on at the house?"

Megan rolled her eyes as she struggled to keep pace with Georgie. "It's a nightmare. Abigail, the widow, came to breakfast. I thought she was genuinely upset, but she could've had a bit of a hangover too. Not quite sure about that, but the conversation was a bit contentious."

"Really? How so?" Georgie asked.

"We don't have any more info than we did yesterday, but people seemed to point immediate fingers this morning. I couldn't believe it. They were talking about Randall's death as if it were a scene from a movie. I honestly felt bad for Abigail. If her grief was real, the conversation was rather insensitive."

"Well, that's not right," Georgie agreed. The pair continued to slowly run the length of the boardwalk, already full of tourists. They passed various shops selling gifts and sundries. As they reached the entrance of the pier, they ran past a series of dart and balloon games. A man holding a microphone called out to them to try a bean bag or a basketball for free. A half- mile later, the pair arrived at the boardwalk midway. Their senses were assailed with the scent of pizza, sausage sandwiches, lemonade, ice cream, funnel cake, fries and sheer adolescent fun.

"If we stop here, I'm going to have to run ten more miles," Megan huffed as she continued down the boards.

Georgie slowed to a walk after another couple blocks. Megan was grateful for the opportunity to stop and catch her breath.

"Don't lock your knees," Georgie said as she checked on her friend. "Walk around a bit so you don't build up lactic acid."

Megan stood up and with one hand on her hip, she walked back and forth on the boardwalk until her breathing evened out. "So, how far was that?"

"About two miles," Georgie said, now breathing normally. "You need to start running again on a regular basis. You'll feel better."

"Thank you for dragging me out," Megan said. "But, I have a feeling there's something more."

"And you would be right," Georgie said with a chuckle.

"So, out with it. What's up?"

"I wanted you to look at the children's amusement park," Georgie said.

Megan knew the larger rides sat towards the edge of the pier and peaked over the water. The children's rides were closer inland and located on the other side of the boardwalk. There were miniature versions of water boat rides, tea cups, a Ferris wheel and a roller coaster. The children also enjoyed a large bounce house, a big green train and games.

With a big smile, Megan recalled memories of Grandma Rose taking her on the rides when she was a young girl. It was a special time for them.

Megan looked back toward her friend. "I had a lot of good times on those rides. Is this a therapy thing to help with my depression?"

"I wish it were," Georgie said. "That would've been a promising idea, but no. We said there were people upset with your father and Douglas Randall after their visit to town so I started asking a few questions."

Megan's eyes snapped to Georgie's face. "And, what did you find out?"

"Do you see the hotel over there?" Georgie pointed to the right.

"Yes, it's been there for years," Megan said while deep breathing.

"Well, the reason they were upset was your father and his friend were loudly discussing how they would knock the hotel down and build expensive condominiums. In addition, their idea was to turn the children's amusement park into tennis courts to serve their clientele. They also planned to cap the boardwalk a few blocks back to ensure there would be ample parking for the private exclusive beach."

"Wow, is that all?" Megan asked with eyes open wide. "That would mean half of the boardwalk shop owners would have to close."

"Or stay open but lose a lot of business," Georgie nodded. "No one can afford to operate at a loss."

Megan moved her hands to her hips and walked in a few tight circles to keep her muscles from cramping up. "I understand how upset everyone would be, but would that be enough reason to kill someone? Especially if it was just talk?"

"A lot of people were talking about Douglas's death this morning in the coffee shop," Georgie said. "They're concerned if your father inherits, he'll find another developer to replace him."

Megan turned to face her friend. "I understand how upsetting my father can be, but don't forget, we don't know anything, yet. Grandma Rose probably put some sort of lifetime clause in the boardwalk or beach area. She loved coming here." Megan turned toward the water, suddenly unable to stop tears from falling down her cheeks.

Georgie walked up from behind and put her hand on her friend's shoulder. "I'm really sorry to upset you, but maybe it's a good idea to work through some of this. I wanted you to know what was being said in town."

Megan wiped her eyes with the heel of her hands. She swallowed hard. "Other than seeing my grandmother and reconnecting with Nick and my friends, coming back to New Jersey has been a nightmare."

"Sometimes we need to move through some tough terrain to move forward," Georgie said. "I have no doubt your grandmother felt her prayers were answered when you returned home to her."

The lump in Megan's throat began to grow again. She remained steadfast in dealing with her grandmother's death, and her father's return, never allowing herself to cry or give in to her feelings of defeat. The bereavement counselor from Cape Shore Hospice had called her several times since her grandmother died. Although Megan didn't answer her previous calls and refused her visits, she left a message on the phone each time which was to let Megan know her feelings would eventually break through and when they did, she should let them flow, tears and all. The counselor explained the process was normal and would help with her thoughts and emotions. When she allowed herself to cry, the guilt, anger, denial and loss Megan felt for her grandmother would process.

Deliberately trying to distract her, Georgie strong armed her friend. "Hey, we have to get ready to run back two miles. C'mon, you're going to stiffen up if we wait too long."

Megan wiped her eyes again and turned to her friend. "You're lucky I ran here. Now you want me to run back?"

"Well, I'm not going to carry you," Georgie said as she started to pull Megan along. They walked for a few feet when Megan stopped at a pizza booth and grabbed one of the paper napkins from the holder on the counter.

"Let me walk for a bit," Megan said. "You don't have to wait for me. I don't want to screw up your morning run."

"Like hell." Georgie fell in step with Megan as they walked down the boardwalk. "I'm sorry if I made you feel miserable. I thought I would be helping by starting to piece together some of the mystery, but now I realize how insensitive that was. You're grieving and I should have thought it through."

"Georgie, it's not your fault. If you want to blame anyone, blame my father. Talk about self-centered and insensitive. He's an ass."

After a few more steps, Georgie turned to Megan. "That's enough walking. Let's go." She grabbed her friend and pulled her along as she started to pick up her pace.

Blowing out a puff of air, Megan pushed off the boards and began to run.

Chapter Forty-Two

"So, what happens now?" Savannah asked as she stood next to Kevin on the porch of Misty Manor. They were standing near a post, watching the waves rush to shore.

"Who the hell knows," Kevin said as he shrugged his shoulders. "The first thing I'd like to do is get back to Texas. Then, I must immediately meet with the lawyers and the board of directors. It's amazing how quickly things can turn around in our lives."

Savannah waited for a few moments and then leaned against Kevin. He looked at her for a moment, then turned back to the ocean.

Reaching around his waist, she softly whispered. "Remember what you told me?"

Kevin looked at her again. "Hmm, not sure. I've said a lot of things."

Savannah nodded. "Yes, you have. Do you remember when we stayed late at the office?"

Kevin looked at her without saying anything.

"Umm, we had a nice long talk on the couch," Savannah prompted him using her fingers to make quotes marks around "on the couch" before she put her arm back around his waist.

Kevin gave a friendly smile as his arm continued to rest on the porch post. "It was a sweet time, Savannah."

"Yes, it was." She hugged him more tightly. "We talked about being together more often, officially being a couple."

"We have fun when we're together," Kevin repeated.

Savannah looked up into his face. "But we could have more fun if we were together all the time, you know, in some sort of meaningful relationship."

Kevin continued to stare out at the ocean and smile. "Savannah, things are going to get a little crazy from now on. I don't know how much of a relationship I can commit to. After all, now that Douglas is gone, I'll be playing a very crucial role in the company. I'll miss him, of course. He was my mentor and the person who got me into the development business. But now that he's gone, I'll have to make his memory proud by stepping into my new role in the company."

Savannah pulled her arm away from Kevin. "And it doesn't sound like there's much room in the new role for me," Savannah said, starting to fume.

"We'll see each other at the office," Kevin said as he winked at her. "You know, on the couch. You understand, right?"

"I'm beginning to," Savannah said. "Very clearly."

Chapter Forty-Three

Megan and Georgie reached the end of the boardwalk and slowed their pace. They began to walk the remaining distance toward Misty Manor.

"My, don't they look cozy?" Georgie asked as they spied Savannah and Kevin on the porch. They watched as Savannah pulled her arm away from Kevin's waist.

"I don't know what he just said to her, but she's not looking very happy," Megan said.

"I didn't realize they were in a relationship. I thought she was an administrative assistant to both partners," Georgie said.

"Supposedly, she is. Although, I've seen Abigail shooting daggers at her from time to time."

"Maybe she's trying to get a promotion the old-fashioned way," Georgie said with a giggle.

"I have no idea and really no interest," Megan said as they approached the porch. Savannah and Kevin had disappeared. Megan placed her foot on one of the steps and leaned forward to stretch her muscles again. "I can't believe how out of shape I am."

"It looks like a fairly nice shape from here," a male voice said from behind.

Megan snapped herself upright and turned around. "Nick! I can't believe you said that."

"I meant it. You have a lovely figure." Nick moved forward, placed his arms around Megan's waist and kissed her on top of the head.

"Well, I guess that's my clue to leave," Georgie said with a laugh.

"Do you have to go?" Megan asked, reaching out for her friend's hand.

Georgie looked at her watch. "Yes, I really do. I should make sure all the lifeguards are getting their break. I normally don't leave the beach when I'm working but I thought it was important I let you know about that information."

Nick's ears perked up. "Oh, really? Anything interesting?"

Georgie looked at Megan. "I'm out of here. You can tell him if you want." The pair watched as Georgie took off and ran back down the boardwalk to the first lifeguard station.

Nick place his arm around Megan's waist. "So, what was that all about? Talk to me."

"Apparently, my father discussed some development plans in front of a group of people who would most likely lose their jobs, their businesses, and possibly their homes as a result."

"Seriously?"

"Yes, and now I can understand why the hotel manager said they were full when Abigail, Savannah, and Kevin looked for a room," Megan explained. "As a bonus, my father and Randall were going to demolish the children's amusement park and turn it into tennis courts and a parking lot."

Nick's eyes opened wide. "Would he really do that?"

Megan looked at Nick to see if he was being sarcastic. After a moment, she said, "If it was profitable, he would do it in a heartbeat."

"You're right. It's no wonder he pissed them off." Nick guided Megan up the porch steps and into the house. When they were inside, he turned to Megan and said, "I'm sorry, but I'm here on business. Can you get your guests to gather? I have some information for them."

Megan was immediately on alert. "You found something, didn't you?"

Nick turned to Megan. He saw the bags under her eyes, her pale cheeks and worry between her brows. He leaned forward and whispered in her ear. "Please don't tell anyone, but the ME is going to label this death a homicide."

Megan looked up at him, with wide open eyes. "He was officially murdered?"

"Shhh," Nick said, placing a finger to his lips. "Don't say anything else."

"Please tell me, what makes them so sure he was murdered?"

"A few things," Nick whispered. "He was fully dressed so he wasn't planning on being in the water as well as the wound on his head." Watching the look on her face, Nick gathered her in his arms and held her to his chest. He whispered in her ear. "I know it's hard to accept. Please, just get everyone down to the parlor without telling them anything. You must promise me to keep this information confidential. Otherwise, you'll compromise the investigation as well as my job." He kissed the top of her head and pulled back.

"You got it," Megan said as she shuddered. "I'll ring the call bell to get them together, but I have to do it the old-fashioned way."

Nick was initially at a loss for words. "I don't know what you mean."

"Watch this," Megan smiled. "I found this the other day." She walked halfway down the hall to the right of the grand staircase. Expensive pieces of antique art decorated the hall and although not worth millions there were valuable paintings brought over from Europe years before. Several paintings were framed with thick damask curtains. Megan pulled back one of the curtains and found a long satin cord. She turned back to see if Nick was watching. Smiling, she pulled the satin cord and the foyer burst into sound with the loud peal of a bell. After a moment or two, she stopped as Nick made his way to the curtain.

"What is this?" Nick asked looking up at the large, brass bell mounted at the top of the curtain.

"It's one of my great-grandfather's voyage bells. Whenever they safely returned home from a trip across the ocean, he was given the ship bell as a memento of his service. If you look closely, you'll see his name engraved on the front of the bell. When I was a child, Grandma Rose would ring this bell to call us to dinner."

"That is a neat call bell." Nick craned his neck to see better. As he was trying to decipher the inscription, voices came from the stairs.

"What's going on? Is everything okay?"

The pair turned to see Abigail standing on the upper landing. Megan noticed Kevin and Savannah coming from different directions. "Everything is fine," Megan said. "Nick would like to meet with us and give an update on the case. Can everyone come down to the parlor?"

Megan watched a flurry of emotions cross over Abigail's face. Finally, she turned, descended the staircase and crossed to the parlor. Megan and Nick watched to see Kevin and Savannah go into the room as well. They heard Savannah whisper, "I hope this means we can get out of this hell hole."

"Where's your father?" Nick asked.

"I have no idea," Megan said as she shrugged her shoulders. "If there wasn't money involved, I'd swear he took off to Europe again."

"Amazing," Nick said as he took another quick look around the downstairs floor before he and Megan followed everyone into the parlor. When they were all seated, Abigail, wide-eyed and anxious asked, "What's going on?"

Nick cleared his throat, buying time, as he decided how to begin. "I don't have a lot of news for you today, except that Chief Davis has asked for everyone to remain in NJ."

"Why are we having this meeting?" Kevin asked, shaking his head in frustration. "My phone is ringing off the hook. I've got a business to run, so do your job and get to the bottom of this so we can leave."

"We know you're anxious to be on your way, and the body hasn't been released by the medical examiner, but we're expecting it to be soon." Nick said as he turned to Abigail. "I'm sorry this is adding to your stress but when a death is unexpected, there has to be a complete investigation."

"I don't understand why," Savannah said as she spread her hands apart. "If it was an accidental drowning, how much of an investigation can there be?"

Megan shook her head in understanding as she recalled the events of a few months ago. "Believe me, in New Jersey, they're always asking questions. They need to sort through everything."

"Has anyone remembered anything more since we talked? Does anyone remember seeing Douglas leave the house? Did he mention he was meeting anyone?" Nick asked as he looked at each guest. They looked at one another, waiting to see if anyone had information to share.

When no one spoke, Nick got up. "Okay, I guess that's all for now. Hopefully, we'll have a definitive answer soon." Nick turned to Abigail. "We'll let you know as soon as we have enough information. Then you can start making funeral arrangements."

Abigail took an extra moment to respond. She appeared almost dazed as she answered, "Thank you. There's a lot to be done to bring Randall home."

Chapter Forty-Four

Andrew Davenport leaned his hand on his Cherrywood desk, thumbing through a pile of paperwork which littered the surface. He had come to his office to prepare for a meeting later in the day with the town council. He reviewed a few documents and found everything in order. The new zoning would be proposed tonight and Andrew wanted to be on top of his game when it was presented. Several years ago, he wouldn't have had to worry, but since the most recent election, the meetings had become more contentious. Each agenda item was challenged by the public, if not by the new council members.

Everyone was on pins and needles since Rose Stanford died. She was a staple in the community and made it her business to keep the town as true to its natural roots as possible. She wanted the beach kept clean and public. But that cost money. Rose was a smart woman and put several initiatives in place to create revenue. Not only did it cover the cost of caring for the beach, it helped to lower taxes for the residents who lived in the community year-round.

Andrew's thoughts were disrupted when he heard a knock on the door. He turned his head in time to watch Chief Davis slowly open the door, enter the room and take a seat in one of the strained leather arm chairs sitting across from the desk.

"Penny for your thoughts? I was knocking for a while out there. Your assistant told me you were in but I was beginning to think otherwise." Davis pulled at his pants so he could cross his leg comfortably.

Andrew looked at the man, wondering why he was paying him an unannounced visit. "Just going over some notes for the meeting tonight. No offense, Chief, but I don't get personal visits from you unless it's bad news. What's going on?"

Davis took a moment. "I know this is a bit awkward, but I need to ask you some questions."

"Jeez, don't make it sound so damn official. Do I need my lawyer?"

"Not unless you think you need a lawyer," Davis said and waited for a reaction. "Are you worried about something?"

Andrew shifted in his chair and threw the pen he was holding on the desk. "What's your question, Chief?"

"I know you're aware we had a drowning on the beach, yesterday."

"Yes, I was informed," Davenport said testily.

"The medical examiner called me this morning. He's ruling the death a homicide," Davis said as he continued to watch the mayor.

Davenport kept his face blank. "It's always unfortunate when we have a death at the beach, especially when it's a tourist. It's bad for business."

"I don't imagine his family is happy about it, either. They don't know it's going to be labeled a homicide," Davis said, sarcastically. "Which will be even worse for business."

"What's your point?"

"Something didn't look right yesterday so we started questioning everyone while their memories were fresh and they didn't have time to compare stories."

"And what does that mean to me?"

"They had quite of bit to say about you issuing threats at Misty Manor the day before yesterday. Seems your concern was specifically directed toward development in Misty Point."

Andrew paled for a moment, then recovered quickly. "I'm the friggin' mayor. People are upset all over town. It's my job to see what's going on."

Davis nodded his head. "I completely agree with you, but from what I was told, it didn't sound like you were worried about any of the town folk."

"I don't care what you heard," Davenport yelled. "If you have something to say, then say it. Otherwise, get out of my office. Don't forget who you work for, Davis. Keep bothering me and I'll have your badge."

Davis remained in his chair and smiled at the mayor. "Sir, where were you night before last, let's say at approximately 10:00 pm?"

Davenport felt his chest go tight with rage. He remembered how his father had chest pain while being questioned several months ago and could only imagine how he felt. "Get out."

"Sir, could you please answer the question?"

Through clenched teeth, Davenport said. "As it happens, I had a meeting."

Davis digested that information. "See, I knew you couldn't be involved." As he got up from his chair he continued, "I'm sure it'll be easy to get us a list of who else was there so we can get corroboration out of the way. Thank you for your cooperation and have a delightful day."

Davenport's face was red with anger. "Get out, now, or I swear this will be your last day at work."

"Of course, Mayor." Davis walked to the door and just as he was getting ready to exit, he turned and asked, "Oh, before I go, I was wondering, how is your son?" Without waiting for an answer, he left the room before the coral paper weight smashed into the door where his head had been seconds before.

Chapter Forty-Five

Marie climbed up the back stairs and placed several grocery bags on a table next to the back door. Misty Manor boasted a beautiful wraparound porch, yet, most of the time, everyone used the front door.

Marie used the back door almost exclusively. There were two rocking chairs on the back side of the porch. The view from those chairs was that of the land behind the house on which sat two small summer cottages and the demolished remains of the other two waiting for removal. Beyond the expansive lawn, was a beautiful stand of trees. Occasionally, Marie would sit in a rocking chair on the North side of the porch, where she could look toward the lighthouse which was located on the point of the town, hence its name, Misty Point. Either way, she enjoyed being alone where she could relax.

Marie unlocked the door and picked up the grocery bags. Filled with meat and vegetables to be prepared, they were quite heavy. She had additional plastic bags which held several round watermelons for dessert. She hoped she would have time to return to the chairs after dinner, but for now she'd have to cook if the guests stayed, invited or uninvited. She loved Misty Manor and at one time had imagined herself living there as the wife of Dean Stanford, before she found out he was seeing other women while they were dating thirty years ago. Having this opportunity to help Megan and enjoy the house was a privilege, although she was sorry Megan had seen nothing but sorrow since she returned to New Jersey.

Marie wanted to stay away from the drama. She was beginning to have panic attacks again. She woke up soaking wet with her heart hammering in her chest. She had to plan soon. Should she tell Megan what she saw that night or was she just creating a nightmare for herself? Chief Davis had left her out of the questioning. Why open herself up to scrutiny if she didn't have to? But still, she wanted to help Megan and be rid of these people as soon as possible.

Chapter Forty-Six

Megan walked along the water near the beach. The warm water lapped around her ankles and the sand was soft, allowing her toes to sink in the sand.

After the meeting in the parlor, she walked Nick to his car. Megan asked him to stay for a while, but he needed to go back to the station to report to Davis. The official report from the medical examiner would be in by now and they had to solidify their information to follow up.

Megan looked up to see the lighthouse in front of her. She would normally cross the lawn and then the beach near Misty Manor, but the memory of Randall's bloated body with one eye left wide open and staring in death was too disturbing for her at the moment. So, she cut off to the left and headed towards the Point until she wound up near the lighthouse.

Billy Conklin, the family lighthouse keeper, continued to live in the small apartment at the base of the lighthouse and as far as Megan was concerned could stay there if he wanted. Although he had strange habits, he was a loyal and devoted family friend.

Megan initially worried about the elderly man living there alone until she found out he was the uncle of Tommy McDonough. Amber and Tommy had been getting more serious lately, even helping each other to support Billy.

Billy must have spied her approaching the lighthouse because he walked outside to greet her as she came near. She waved as she recalled memories of him being around for most of her early life. He loved Grandma Rose and helped support the family in all ways possible, but did so on his own time and in his own way. He relished being a hermit which is why Megan was surprised when he came out to greet her.

"Hi, how are you?" Megan asked as she made her way toward the grizzled, elderly man.

Billy simply nodded as he rubbed the stubble on his chin and waited for her to reach him.

Megan shielded her eyes from the sun and stopped when she neared the man. "Are you okay?"

"I'm okay, but I was wondering how you folks are up at the house," Billy said as he squinted his eyes and nodded. He had permanent crow's feet from years of doing the same thing.

Megan looked at him for a few minutes before answering. "Everything is a bit unsettled right now, ever since Randall Douglas drowned. Did you see the ambulance a few days ago?"

"I did and I talked to the police officer a few hours after that," Billy said. "But I didn't hear nothing else since then so I was wondering if they found the other person."

Surprised, Megan frowned and tilted her head. "What other person?"

"I told the young officer that there were two people out on the jetty that night. I couldn't tell if they were both men or a man and a woman but there were two of them. I'm pretty sure they were drinking cause the light kept flashing off the bottle."

"Wow. Are you sure?"

"Sure as I am we're standing here having this conversation," Billy said, rubbing his arm. "Maybe the police don't want anyone to know they're on to them."

"But who could've been out there with him?" Megan asked again.

"Don't know that, little one." Megan smiled at the nickname Billy use to call her. She hadn't heard that name in many years.

"I don't know if they identified who it was," Megan said. "Nick didn't mention it to me."

"Then it would be best if you didn't mention it to anyone else," Billy said. "I feel more trouble in my bones so make sure you stay safe, you hear?"

"I will," Megan said, feeling a bit of anxiety. "Thank you for warning me." In an awkward move, Megan burst forward and hugged the man. "I never said so, but thank you for everything you've done, Billy. For me and for Grandma Rose."

He looked down at his feet and shuffled a bit. "Alright now, little one. You go along, but I'll be watching from the lighthouse.

Tommy gave me one of these fancy phones so if I see something I can call him. And I will, if I do see something."

Megan smiled, despite feeling chilled. "Okay, thanks Billy. Promise me you'll take care of yourself."

Billy cracked an aged smile. "I've done okay so far. I'll be fine." He then turned and limped back into the lighthouse.

Chapter Forty-Seven

Megan spent the rest of her walk in deep thought. Why hadn't Nick told her there was a second person on the jetty with Randall? Was the killer staying in Misty Manor? She was determined to give Nick a call as soon as she had some privacy.

Megan entered through the front door. She looked around, but the only person she found was Marie, who was busy searching the kitchen.

"What are you doing?" Megan asked, watching Marie move about.

Startled, Marie looked up and laughed. "Looking for something. I think I'm losing my mind."

"Why?"

"I brought several bags of groceries into Misty Manor about an hour ago," Marie said. "There was a sale on round watermelons so I bought four of them to carve for dinner. I left the kitchen for two minutes to get something else from my car and now I only have three watermelons."

"Is it possible you only brought three into the house?"

"Absolutely not. I had them all on the counter an hour ago."

"Maybe someone was very hungry," Megan suggested.

"I was only out of the room for two minutes," Marie said while shaking her head.

"Don't worry about it," Megan said. "We have other fish to fry. Where is everyone?"

Shrugging, Marie frowned. "I have no idea."

"That's okay, just relax. I'm going up to my room for a bit."

"Fine, but dinner will be on the table in forty minutes."

"You got it," Megan said as she left the kitchen. She was eager to call Nick. Not seeing anyone else, she ran up the grand staircase to the third floor. When she reached the landing, she immediately stopped when she heard hushed whispers down the hall from her bedroom. No one was staying on the third floor except her. Anxiety engulfed her as she crept down the hall to find out who was there.

Slowly, she stepped forward trying to be as quiet as possible so whoever was up here would not hear her. She reached the farthest bedroom and peered around the door frame to find Abigail Douglas and her father rummaging in the closet. It became apparent to Megan that nothing other than blankets and extra pillows were stored there as she watched them search the shelves and a small ledge.

Megan's bedroom had been the only room on the third floor she remembered being in use for most of her years. When she was a small child and there were family parties or many relatives visiting the beach, she recalled a visitor or two staying there, but the memories were hazy. She couldn't imagine why they were searching this room. Had they searched hers as well? Anger swelled up in her as she planted herself in the doorway. "Can I help you with something here?"

The pair were clearly surprised by her voice and jumped at her question. Her father snapped upright and hit his head on the edge of the shelf in the closet. As he turned around, she said, "What the hell are you doing in here?"

Abigail's mouth moved but no words came out. Once Dean recovered from being surprised, he took the offensive. "What's it to you what we're doing? We don't answer to you."

Megan clenched her teeth. "You have no business being up here. Grandma Rose wouldn't want the two of you up here and I want you both out of here now."

"You can't order me around," Dean said, his face turning red and his hands clenching into fists. "Misty Manor is mine, now."

After years of watching her father's self-centered, narcissistic personality, fury ignited in her. She stood as tall as she could and confronted him with all her strength. Through gritted teeth she said, "Nothing is yours until I hear Teddy say so. Damn you and your selfish ways. You weren't here for your mother, your wife or for me and I'll be damned if I'm going to let you walk in here and start screwing with Misty Manor just to satisfy yourself and another damn girlfriend."

Dean raised his hand and swung to slap his daughter across the face. He would have succeeded if Abigail hadn't caught his arm and pulled it down. "Stop it, stop it both of you." Abigail placed herself between Megan and her father. She turned to Megan. "I'm sorry this happened. You should know I'm an antique dealer and your father seemed to remember some wonderful things being in the house, but he couldn't find them. Dean wanted to show them to me before I returned to Texas. He thought they may be in the attic, but there's a lock. We thought the key might be stored here somewhere."

Megan remembered Grandma Rose telling her Tommy had helped her place most of the valuables in the attic years ago, in preparation for Hurricane Sandy. She also had a new latch and extra security lock placed on the door in case she didn't have access to Misty Manor immediately after the storm. After years of living near the beach, she was aware of what type of pilfering could happen when beach houses were unattended. Megan knew where the key to the lock was stored but she'd never tell them.

"I know she used to keep the old key up here. I remember her storing it in this closet. Megan, do you know where the new key is?" Dean screamed at her.

Megan smiled at them, shrugged and said, "I have no idea where it is. Grandma Rose was not in her right mind at the end. It could be anywhere."

Abigail turned toward Dean. "I'm too upset about my husband to be worrying about any antiques right now. I know you said you had something special up here that could be worth a lot of money and when you find it, you can call me in Texas, but I've had enough for now. Plus, I don't need to make extra money, considering I have a business interest to take care of. I just want to make my husband's funeral arrangements and get the hell out of New Jersey. Please, let's go." Abigail crossed her arms and waited for him to leave the room before she moved.

After staring at the two of them, Dean pushed Megan as he brushed by her to leave the room. He turned around to face her and said through clenched teeth, "That's fine. By the way, Teddy did call today and he plans to be here day after next to read the will. From what he's said to me already, you better plan on having your ass out of Misty Manor within seconds after he's done or I'll make sure you wish you'd never come back." Without waiting for Abigail, he stormed down the hall and headed for the grand staircase.

Abigail turned to find Megan clenching her jaw. "I'm so sorry I was part of that. I assure you, your father suggested we look."

Megan stared at Abigail, not sure if she should believe her or not. "I don't know who suggested what, but I do want to thank you for protecting me."

Abigail gave her a sad smile, nodded her head and left the room.

Chapter Forty-Eight

Tears flooded Megan's face as she made her way toward her bedroom. Grandma Rose always protected her as she was growing up. She shielded Megan from her father's abuse and provided as much love as she could to replace his anger. Megan couldn't believe Rose would abandon her now, but if her father's words were true, Megan would gladly leave. She wouldn't be able to stand by and watch him destroy Grandma Rose's legacy.

Wiping her face with her hand, she entered her bedroom and made her way across the room. She almost jumped onto the bed but stopped immediately as fear gripped her heart. On her pillow was the missing watermelon. A note was pinned to the fruit as sticky juice leaked over her favorite pillow shams and comforter. Several ants were already busy collecting their dinner from the juice that had seeped to the floor. Shaking, she approached the head of the bed to read the note which was held in place by a carving knife.

STOP ASKING QUESTIONS OR YOU WILL BE NEXT

The note was typed, in block letters and large font. She recognized the paper as the same stock from her grandmother's small office in the downstairs hall. Megan struggled to remember if she had locked that door. She remembered checking all the doors when her father first arrived with Randall Douglas and was certain it had been locked. Who else had keys to the rooms in the house? Her heart began to beat rapidly and she felt dizzy. It was most likely her father had keys and he was an angry man, but would he leave a note as threatening as this for his daughter? It had obviously been done before Megan found them in the bedroom.

Megan backed up to the other side of the room and pulled her phone out of the pocket of her shorts. Her fingers shaking, she fumbled with the screen as she tried to call Nick. After several rings she heard his voice, "Hello?"

"Nick, can you please come over? Can you get here fast?"

"Megan, calm down. What's going on?"

She began crying as the shock wore off. "Nick, please. Someone left a threatening message on my bed with a carving knife. I'm scared."

"Don't touch a thing," Nick said as he grabbed his keys and ran out to his car. "I'll be there in five minutes. Stay on the phone with me." He threw the phone on the seat beside him as the speaker came on over the Bluetooth in the car.

"Who would do this?" Megan said. "There's a note and I recognize the paper from my grandmother's office, but I swear I had the door locked."

"Who else had keys?" Nick asked. "Is the door locked now?"

"I don't know," Megan said. "I'm afraid to go down there by myself."

Nick kept talking to Megan as he drove toward her home. He wanted to keep her distracted so she wouldn't become hysterical. Parking the Camaro, he ran up the front steps of Misty Manor, opened the front door and ran up the grand staircase. He continued to talk as he ran down the hall and into her room.

Megan was standing with her arms crossed over her chest, resting her smart phone on her upper arm as she spoke. When she saw Nick, she dropped her phone on her dresser and allowed him to crush her to his chest. He smoothed her hair and held her tight until she stopped shaking. Over her head, he tried to look at the watermelon on her bed, the pink juice staining the white linens underneath.

Finally, he held her away from him and stared at her face. "Hey, you're okay. Everything is good. Someone is just trying to scare you." Nick used his smart phone to dial the station and called for a tech to come to the house to check for fingerprints. He then used his phone to take several photos of the watermelon and note, being careful not to touch anything.

Megan watched him and then scowled. "You didn't tell me there were two people on the jetty that night. There could be a killer staying here, right now."

Surprise registered on Nick's face. "How did you find out about that?"

"I went for a walk and ran into Billy. He told me what he saw."

"I'm sorry but I couldn't tell you. It may have compromised the investigation. We don't release all the details for a reason. Please don't tell anyone you know that."

Their conversation stopped abruptly when a man appeared in her doorway. He carried a kit and had a plastic jacket for protection. Nick waved him into the room.

"Hey, Nick. I knocked on the front door. Someone let me in and told me you were waiting up here."

"Thanks for getting here so fast. I wanted to see if there was a chance of recovering any prints off that knife."

The tech looked over at the bed and smiled. "Looks like a terminal melon."

Nick shot him a look until he turned and approached the bed. He placed his kit on a safe surface on the wooden floor and got to work. He dusted the note, the knife and even part of the melon. He then placed a clear sticky sheet over the same areas to see if anything showed up. Once he was done, he collected everything in labeled bags to carry them back to the police station.

Megan and Nick made their way downstairs and she promised to stay in the parlor until he came back for her. While she waited, Nick talked to Marie and looked for anyone else he could find. No one appeared to be home and he certainly wasn't expecting a confession. Nick checked Grandma Rose's small office and found the door unlocked. Anyone could have been in the room.

As he was walking toward the parlor, there was a knock on the front door. Nick veered off and opened the door to find Georgie, Amber and Tommy. He called his friends inside and together, they all entered the house and made their way to a surprised Megan.

"I'm so glad to see you guys. What are you doing here?" She jumped up off the easy chair and raced toward them.

Georgie spoke first. "Nick called us to come over. He thought you could use a little company."

Nick turned to Megan. "I have to get back to the station but I knew you'd be too nervous to stay here alone."

"You got that right," Megan said. "I was going to try to talk you into staying one way or another."

Nick laughed. "That sounds like it would have been lovely but unfortunately, I have to get back."

Tommy chimed in. "We ordered a couple of pies and some cold beer so we could hang for a while."

"Wow, I think Marie made dinner," Megan said as she looked at her friends.

"That's okay," Georgie said. "Let her feed your guests. We'll hang in the kitchen with the pizza and beer."

Megan laughed. "That's the best offer I've had all day."

Chapter Forty-Nine

Two hours later, the group had finished two pizzas and half a case of cold beer. Georgie chided her friend. "Jeez, I thought you said you didn't have an appetite."

Megan shrugged. "I can't explain it, maybe it's stress eating."

Laughing, Tommy picked up a fresh bottle and popped the cap.

"I can understand that," Amber said as she sipped at her single low-carb beer.

Megan polished off her last piece of pizza crust and wiped her hands.

"I couldn't believe it when I saw your father last night at The Clamshell," Amber said.

Megan paused for a moment. "Wait, what did you say?"

Amber looked at her friend. "Tommy and I were at The Clamshell last night. He was making arrangements for the group to sing there again."

"Yeah, I finished talking to Foster and I turn around and your father is sitting there," Tommy added.

"But, you'll never believe who he was with," Amber said, opening her eyes for emphasis.

Megan shook her head. "I have no idea, but I'm not surprised. It there's a party in town, he'll find it."

Amber grabbed Megan's arm and looked at her friend. "Are you ready for this? He was actually having drinks with that shrew, Fran Stiles."

Megan's head whipped around. "What?"

Amber nodded. "You heard me. She's the one who messed up your car a month ago."

"Not to mention who almost killed my grandmother with neglect while stealing her things," Megan said, her face turning red. "I'll bet she has keys to every room in the house."

Georgie took another bite of pizza. "I thought you changed the locks when you booted her out of here."

"I changed the lock on the front door, but not every lock in the place. And if you remember, I caught her in Grandma Rose's office the first day I arrived here."

Nodding her head, Georgie said, "I remember how upset you were."

Megan chewed her lip. "I can't believe he met her at a bar. He apparently has absolutely no couth."

"Or taste, either," Amber murmured, before looking up. "Oh, did I say that out loud?" The group broke into laughter which helped to lighten the mood.

Eventually, the group drifted out to the front porch. As her friends got ready to leave, Megan became quiet. They hugged, said goodbye and she thanked them for keeping her company for a while. As they walked down the steps, Georgie turned to her and said, "I'll be back in a minute."

Surprised, Megan nodded her head and took a seat in one of the rocking chairs behind her. She listened to her friends laugh as they made their way across the lawn. Amber and Tommy had planned on taking a moonlit walk on the boardwalk. Megan couldn't help noticing it was a beautiful night. The air was warm and she could smell the salty air off the ocean. For a moment, she felt alone and wished Nick were beside her.

"Alright, I'm all set," Georgie said as she returned to the porch laden with bags and blankets.

"What's all that?" Megan asked trying to make sense of her friend.

Georgie laughed. "I may be an adult in age, but when it comes to sleepovers, I still need a special blanket and pillow."

"Sleepover?"

"Just like the old days," Georgie said. "Did you think we would leave you alone with those freaks after a find like that?"

Megan couldn't help laughing despite herself. "I had no idea, but I'm glad I have company."

"The first thing to decide is what bedroom we're sleeping in because it's not going to be your room."

Megan nodded. "You're right. I guess I just wasn't planning on sleeping ever again."

Now it was Georgie's turn to chuckle. "You may be able to get away with that, but I have to sleep. So, let's go upstairs and pick one out."

Megan picked up the pile of blankets while Georgie shouldered a back pack. Together, the two of them headed inside the house and up the stairs.

Chapter Fifty

Megan lay awake. She stared at the wall in front of her, her eyes having adjusted to the darkness. Lying beside her, Georgie softly snored. After they chose where to stay, Megan and Georgie spent time cleaning up Megan's bedroom. They stripped the bed which now had fingerprint dust and debris stuck to the watermelon juice and threw the linens in the washing machine. Several more ants had joined the feast so after cleaning the area, they washed the bed and floor thoroughly and let it dry.

Megan had a tough time choosing another room to sleep in. Misty Manor hosted eighteen bedrooms, several of which were occupied by the unwelcome guests on the second floor. The only room in use on the third floor was Megan's. Megan briefly thought of sleeping in Grandma Rose's room but couldn't bring herself to go there. She wanted to keep the room exactly as it was when Rose passed away.

The girls finally choose one of the other bedrooms on the third floor, making sure to avoid the one Dean and Abigail had been rummaging through earlier. They each had another beer while they dusted and prepared to go to sleep. It was nearing the wee hours of the morning, but Megan was still wide awake. She kept mentally reviewing the events of the day and searching for clues as to who could have put the watermelon in her room. Did they really mean her harm or were they just trying to scare her?

Megan chided herself and resolved to say prayers until she fell asleep. As she began to drift off, she heard a noise in the hall. Her eyes snapped open and her heart raced as she listened intently for another sound. Her stomach in knots, she trembled as she strained to hear.

Within a minute, she heard another noise. Afraid to move, she turned ever so slightly and whispered, "Georgie?" Megan felt bad she would have to wake her friend, but she was scared.

"I hear it," Georgie whispered.

Relief flooded Megan and she was glad she wasn't alone. "You do?"

"Sure do," Georgie whispered. "Don't make any noise. Someone may be looking for you in your room. Of course, they won't find you there, but they have no idea where you choose to stay tonight."

"Can you friggin' believe this?"

The pair listened for a few more minutes but didn't hear anything. As they began to relax, they heard another loud thump in the hall. Something had been dropped on the floor, the culprit whispering a string of curse words.

Megan's heart thudded in her chest. "What should we do?"

"I'm tempted to open the door and see who the hell is out there," Georgie said. "Do you recognize the voice?"

Megan shook her head in the dark. "No, I can't tell if it's a man or woman."

"Who would be your best guess if you had to choose someone?" Georgie asked.

"I don't know, but I caught Abigail Douglas up here twice searching the rooms. Apparently, my father told her there were valuables here and he was determined to cash in. No sentimentality there."

"I don't want to say anything because whatever I say about your father is going to be ugly."

Megan was quiet for a few moments. "Georgie, I have an idea."

"Uh, oh," Georgie thought. "Here it comes."

"What if we wait until Abigail goes to breakfast tomorrow and then search her room?"

"Why would we want to do that?"

"Because if she's been stealing things, they'll probably be stored in her luggage. Maybe, we'll find some useful intel about Douglas, too."

"I don't know if that's a good idea," Georgie said as she slowly got up and made her way to the door.

"What are you doing?" Megan whispered, becoming alarmed.

"I'm finding out who's playing games up here." Georgie turned the old-fashioned door knob and opened the door a crack. Using one eye, she peered out into the hall. Small wall sconces provided a dim reprieve from the inky dark.

"Georgie, please be careful," Megan called out. She crept up to the door behind her friend. They opened the door a bit wider and could see a figure at the end of the hall. Without light, they couldn't tell if it was male or female. Before they could snap on the hall lights, the figure quickly turned and fled down the stairs.

Chapter Fifty-One

"Why didn't you call me last night?" Nick bellowed through the phone.

"And say what?" Megan asked. "A dark, shadowy figure was roaming the hall?"

"What if someone was looking specifically for you?" Nick asked. "Megan, I don't know what the hell is going on over there, but I'm beginning to think it would be safer to pull you out of there."

"So they can run around doing whatever they want?" Megan asked as Georgie walked into the bedroom brushing her wet hair. There had been no further noise during the night and both girls finally fell into a restless sleep. As soon as Georgie left to take a shower, Megan called Nick to let him know what happened. "Just hurry and finish your investigation so they can get the hell out of here."

"What if it's not them? What if it's your father?"

Megan was quiet as she came to a decision. "As soon as Teddy finishes reading the will, I'll be out of here. There's no sense in me staying here."

Nick hesitated for a second. "I have some room. You know, if you need a place to stay for a while."

Megan smiled and was glad Nick couldn't see her blushing. "Thanks. I'll think it over." Clearing her throat, she continued. "In the meantime, Georgie said she can stay another night. She has to check on her lifeguards and then she'll come back this afternoon.

"We have a few more things to track down, but I'll be stopping by there this morning. Do not isolate yourself this morning. Get out of the house or stay with Marie until I get there."

"Nick, I...."

"Promise me," Nick bellowed. "Don't do anything stupid. I want someone to know where you are at all times."

"I'm not going anywhere," Megan said.

"Promise me, Megan."

Shifting her phone, she reluctantly agreed.

Chapter Fifty-Two

"Georgie, stay and have breakfast with me," Megan said as they made the bed and straightened the room.

"Sure, if you go for another four-mile run with me," Georgie said and immediately laughed when she saw Megan's face. "Even then, I can only have yogurt for breakfast."

"There may be a time when we can run each morning like old times, but I need to get back into shape. Let me start small and build."

"Hey, there are a couple of 5K's around the area next week. Let's register together. Maybe we can drag Amber along as well. It'll be fun."

They walked down the hall and descended the grand staircase. "Let's ask Amber before we sign up," Megan said, her mood tanking as the reality of her situation sunk back in.

"C'mon, let's get coffee. I could use a good dose of caffeine after last night."

"Marie usually puts out a nice breakfast on the sideboard." The pair walked into the dining room but the table was bare. "That's strange," Megan said. "She didn't say anything about not being around today."

"Well, I smell coffee somewhere, so let's go check the kitchen."

They walked into the kitchen and saw a fresh carafe of coffee on the counter, cream and sugar off to the side. There was also a platter of Danish, pastries and rolls with butter and jelly.

The girls fixed themselves a cup of coffee and sat at the kitchen table. Silently, they looked around the empty room and made faces at each other. Georgie shrugged. "Where is everyone?"

"I have no idea," Megan said. "Do you think our friend visited any other rooms? She felt her stomach clench with anxiety. She did not want to worry about the health and welfare of strangers in her house, but she wanted to make sure everyone was accounted for. The girls continued to sip their coffee and nibble on a croissant.

Within ten minutes, they were relieved when the group of guests ambled into the kitchen, looking for breakfast. Abigail was quiet, Kevin looked angry and Savannah was agitated. The girls watched each of their faces to see if any of them could have been in the hallway last night, but nothing seemed obvious.

Abigail approached the counter and poured herself a cup of coffee while the others waited. Savannah rolled her eyes and made a face, hoping to hurry Abigail along. Kevin grabbed one donut to put in his mouth and another to eat a few minutes later.

Savannah finally poured her coffee, then turned toward the table. She looked around for a moment, then addressed Megan. "I don't know where the cook is, but do you have any cinnamon?"

Megan was proud she controlled herself. She fought the urge to point out, once again, they were not staying at a bed and breakfast, nor a hotel, or a public establishment of any kind. They were staying at a rundown Grand Victorian home, which up until several days ago, sported nothing but a can of tuna and some stale crackers.

"I'm sorry, but we seem to be all out of cinnamon."

Savannah's face clouded. She grabbed her coffee cup and left the room. As she left, they heard her greet Dean in the hall so everyone was accounted for except Marie. Megan decided to press Marie as soon as she saw her. She was hiding something and Megan wanted to know what it was.

Georgie's voice brought her out of her reverie. "Listen, I really have to get going. Today is supposed to be the last nice day of the week so I expect the beach to be full. I want to make sure all the lifeguard stations are fully staffed."

"Sure," Megan said. "I'll walk you to the front door." As they left the kitchen, Megan whispered, "I really appreciate you staying here last night. It meant the world to me."

"No sweat," Georgie said. "I'll see you tonight. I know you said Nick will be here later, so I think you'll be fine today."

"Yeah, I just have to find Marie." Megan watched from the porch as Georgie crossed to the boardwalk and began a light jog toward the center of town.

Megan's cell phone began to ring as she watched Georgie disappear along the boards. "Hello?"

"Megan, it's me, Marge."

Megan clutched the phone tighter and held it close to her ear. As she talked she walked along the wraparound porch so she wouldn't be overheard. "Hi, Marge. Did you find anything?"

"Sure did," Marge said, pride apparent in her voice. "Thanks for the tip and you're getting credit as our confidential informant for this one."

"That's rich. I can only wonder how they feel about that at the top."

"Not our problem, right now," Marge pointed out. "Anyway, I'm glad I got you this morning. As you suggested, we're putting out a push notification to all our subscribers within the hour, but I wanted to let you know what I found before you read about it on social media."

"Sounds like something much better than I expected," Megan said as waited for the information.

"We did some digging," Marge said. "Let me pick up my notes. I've got to put my glasses on, too." After a brief silence, she began to read. "As you know, Douglas Development is a construction company known to buy property and turn it into executive, luxury get-away destinations. The new developments are usually over the top glamorous but they're built to accommodate the rich, *I'm entitled and too famous to be around you* crowd. They usually build near scenic areas and highlight amenities such as golf courses and fancy pools."

"That sounds about right," Megan said. "I believe they've made a lot of money that way."

"There's the rub," Marge said, obviously pleased with herself.

"What rub?

"Apparently, their last two deals were stinkers," Marge said, turning pages. "From an inside source, they're overdrawn with their bank to the tune of sixty million dollars."

"What?" Megan was shocked when she heard the news.

"You heard me," Marge said. "If they were looking for a big deal, it would be one which had the potential to bail them out of the trouble they're in now. It's bad enough they lost money, but the last development appears to have been built over some sort of biohazard."

"What? How did that happen?"

"Who knows, but someone wasn't watching the paperwork. Apparently, the development is gorgeous, but carcinogens appear to be suddenly leaking out of the ground."

"Wow, I'm kind of shocked to hear that," Megan said. "I wonder if the people here know all that. You wouldn't think so by the way they act."

"Maybe it's all bluff," Marge said. "By the way, Ed says hi. He misses you and specifically said to tell you that if you come back to Detroit, he intends to get you back on the paper."

Megan smiled. "Thanks, Marge. Tell him I need to sort out a few things in New Jersey before I can move on, but I appreciate the offer."

"He misses you a lot," Marge said. "So, try to come for a visit now and then."

"I will," Megan promised.

"So, we're breaking the story very soon and I'm sure the big papers are going to follow our lead as soon as they can confirm. I'd probably stay away from your phone unless you recognize our number," Marge said.

"Thank for the heads up," Megan said.

Marge paused for a minute before asking, "Do you have any updates for me?"

"No, not really," Megan said. "I'm still getting over the shock that they're insolvent."

"What do you know about the life insurance?" Marge asked.

"Nothing really," Megan said. "I don't know who inherits or how big the policy may be."

"It should be interesting," Marge said. "Maybe this guy thought he was worth more dead than alive."

"Or someone else thought he was worth more dead than alive."

"True. Is there any other tidbit we can add to the story?"

Megan argued with herself about what she should say. She didn't want to offer any information which would cause Misty Manor or the Stanford name to be dragged through the mud. But Megan also knew how important informational relationships were. You tell me yours and I'll tell you mine when it came to secrets. Technically, she had to release something to thank Marge for the update.

"I don't know if this is significant," Megan started.

"Yes?" Marge's voice was full of excitement.

"All I can tell you is the medical examiner has not officially released the body and the police have asked the family not to leave the state."

"Really?"

"Yes, but I don't know what they're looking at or suspicious of," Megan blurted out, perhaps a bit too quickly.

"That's okay, it's a great start," Marge said. "I know where to go from here, but if you hear anything about a life insurance policy or someone looking forward to coming in to some money, you'll let me know?"

"Absolutely," Megan said with a promise. After another few words, Marge rang off. Megan put her phone in her pocket and was happy when she turned around and found she was still alone on the porch. She had no clue who owned most of the company now. Megan got the impression Kevin Shaw thought he was in charge, but she wasn't counting Abigail out either. And did either one of them know the company was bankrupt?

Chapter Fifty-Three

Megan made her way back through the foyer to look for Marie. It was unusual for her not to be in the kitchen in the morning and she normally told Megan her schedule if she was going elsewhere.

She checked the kitchen to no avail. As she planned to walk upstairs to Marie's room she heard someone outside the door and was relieved when Nick poked his head in. Megan grabbed him by the arm, crossed the porch and guided him down the front steps.

"Let's go for a walk," Megan said, as she pulled him after her across the lawn and toward the beach.

"It's a beautiful day for a walk," Nick said.

"It sure is," Megan said as she continued to lead him down the beach toward the Point. They stopped to remove their shoes and socks. The warm, blue water splashed around their ankles as they waded by the ocean's edge. When they reached the Point, Megan pulled Nick toward the gazebo which was situated on a rocky ledge in front of the lighthouse and overlooking the water.

They walked inside, out of the sun and sat down on the bench which faced the ocean. With the waves breaking against the base of the rocks, the ocean breeze in their face, and beautiful scenery of boats and small yachts parading in the ocean, the gazebo was gorgeous and the two were temporarily lost in the scene before them.

"This is lovely," Nick said, with a questioning look, "but I wanted to see what was happening with our guests."

"Well, I just got off the phone with one of my old news friends. You're never going to believe what I just heard."

Nick laughed despite himself at Megan's excitement. "Okay, tell me about it."

"I will," Megan said with a satisfied smile. "I found out Douglas Development is totally insolvent and possibly facing a class action lawsuit as well."

"That's interesting," Nick said. "That's more than we found out."

"I'm not sure who is affected most by all that," Megan said. "I guess it depends on who's in charge of the business now. Also, we're watching to see who the beneficiary of his life insurance is and how much it pays out."

"You'll share your information?"

"Of course, I want to clear this up as soon as possible," Megan said. "Have the police come up with any other clues?" `

"None that I can share. The autopsy showed he wasn't drunk so if he met someone out on the jetty, it was purposeful. Also, the glass in his head wound has been confirmed to be from a wine bottle, but we haven't been able to find a piece large enough to get prints from to identify anyone. Any other trace was washed away by the salt water."

Megan stared out at the ocean. "So, who would kill him like that? It doesn't sound like it was premeditated. If it was, I think someone would choose a murder weapon more sophisticated than a wine bottle."

"I agree, it sounds like it wasn't planned," Nick said. "Do you think your father could have done it? Maybe Randall told Dean that Douglas Development wouldn't be able to offer anything for Misty Manor or the town after all. Would your father react like that?"

Megan laughed. "I guess this would normally be the time I would defend my father's motives and intentions, but I can't do that. He's a real ass and it's possible he could have done it."

"You've been hanging around these people for the last couple of days," Nick pointed out. "Who would you list as your best suspect assuming it was one of your house guests and not a random killing?"

Megan thought for a few seconds, then shrugged. "I don't know. Abigail's grief seemed genuine. His partner, Kevin, doesn't seem like a nice guy. He complains about having so much responsibility for the business now, but he seems happy he's gotten a promotion of sorts. I don't know if he knows all about the money and lawsuit. Maybe he doesn't know the company is in bad shape."

"That's fair," Nick said. "I'm going back to Davis with this info and see if he can get any mileage out of it. Anything else new going on?"

Megan paused for a few seconds before she spoke. "For one thing, I can't find Marie."

"What?" Nick asked as he looked at Megan. He was trying to concentrate on the case, but couldn't help noticing how beautiful her hair looked, blowing in the ocean breeze.

"I can't find Marie," Megan said. "She's usually in the kitchen but she wasn't there today. She had coffee and breakfast all laid out on the kitchen counter, meaning she must've been at Misty Manor earlier this morning, but I haven't seen her all day. I can't imagine her leaving without telling me, but the was food set out, so she clearly didn't intend to stay."

"No note on the counter about going to the store?"

"Not that I saw, but it's possible I missed it," Megan acknowledged. "I have to check for her as soon as I get back."

"There's something else you're not telling me, isn't there?" Nick asked, watching her face.

Megan shrugged as she looked at the ocean. "I don't know, but I think she knows something and she's holding back. She almost told me something the other night and we were interrupted. I haven't been alone with her since then. But we really need to talk to her."

"As soon as we find her, we will," Nick said, pushing back his hair. "I hear Teddy is finally coming tomorrow to read your grandmother's will."

"Apparently, everyone knows except me," Megan said. She hugged her arms in front of her chest and turned toward the ocean. "I don't understand why he didn't call me."

"Maybe he doesn't want to upset you," Nick said. "Everyone knows how close you were to your grandmother and how concerned you've been."

"Could be. I guess we'll find out tomorrow," Megan said with a wry smile.

"See, you're upset now. There's no need to worry, I'm here," Nick said as she placed his arms around her and kissed her on the cheek.

Chapter Fifty-Four

Abigail sat in the rocking chair facing the ocean. She watched the ocean water ebb and flow, crashing on the sand and pulling out again, leaving small eddies of water as if they were fingertips, clinging to the shore.

"Pretty sight, isn't it?"

Abigail looked up to see Kevin standing to her left. He was smiling down at her although Abigail had no idea if his visage was friendly or poised. She looked up at him and nodded. "It sure is different from Texas."

"Let's hope we can get back there soon," Kevin said, nodding as he looked at the water.

An awkward silence filled the air for a minute or two until Abigail looked up and said, "You have something on your mind, Kevin?"

He nodded and crossed behind her, sitting in the rocking chair to her left. "Abigail, we haven't had time to talk since Randall, ah…"

"Yes, I was wondering when we would have this conversation," Abigail said as she continued to gaze out at the water.

Kevin turned to her. "First, you know how sorry I am about Randall. I'll admit we've had differences over the last year or two, but he didn't deserve to die that way."

"And exactly what way is that?"

Kevin fumbled for a moment. "You know, drowning like that."

Abigail looked over at him. "The police must have found something, but they're holding back."

"I have no idea what they found and what they didn't," Kevin said, his voice becoming tight.

"I called my lawyers," Abigail said. "They have another forty-eight hours and then I'm out of here. Either they produce something and arrest us or we leave."

"Hell, I'm ready to leave when you are," Kevin said. "Have you heard from anyone else on the Board yet?"

"No one and it's starting to bother me. I'm beginning to believe the company affairs will not be what we expect," Abigail said in a faint voice.

Kevin was silent for a moment. "Speaking of which, Abigail, I've been meaning to ask what you expect. I mean, I've had a certain legal relationship with this company for several years now, but I have to admit I've never really seen anything in writing."

"What exactly were you hoping for?" Abigail asked.

"As a partner in the company, my lawyer will want bank accounts, investments, holdings, shareholders, the company annual plan, profit/loss statements. Basically, everything."

Abigail chuckled, forcing momentum into her rocking chair. "So, he never told you the details, eh?"

Kevin was clearly becoming agitated. "I don't know the answer to that. Maybe he did. How do I know what I don't know?"

"The die has been cast," Abigail whispered, almost to herself. "I'm sure everything will be out in the open soon enough."

Kevin turned toward the ocean. "Fine Abigail, we'll play it your way, for now, but expect something different when we get back home."

Chapter Fifty-Five

After heading back from the Point, Megan and Nick climbed up the porch stairs of Misty Manor and entered through the foyer. Finding no one in the parlor, they walked towards the kitchen. Before they arrived, the tantalizing smell of a roast greeted them.

"I don't know if it's Marie but it smells like whoever's cooking knows what they're doing," Nick said as they stepped toward the kitchen.

"I didn't realize I was so hungry," Megan said. "Dinner smells delicious."

When they entered the kitchen, they found Marie at the counter whipping up a large bowl of mashed potatoes. The roast was cooling on the counter and a steaming bowl of green beans already sat on the table. Gravy, rolls and salad rounded out the meal.

"Marie, I'm so happy to find you here," Megan said. "I couldn't find you earlier. You had me worried."

Marie looked up at the pair standing in the doorway of the kitchen. She stopped mashing and wiped her hands on an apron around her waist. "I'm sorry about that. I had an important doctor's appointment and I didn't get a chance to tell you before I left."

"Oh, maybe if you left a note?"

"No offense, but there's no way I'm going to leave a note with personal information laying around this house right now." Marie said, raising her eyebrows for emphasis.

Megan shook her head in agreement. "I understand and I'm not trying to pry. I was just worried when I couldn't find you, especially with all the weird things going on around here. Is everything okay?"

Marie shrugged. "I don't have the test results back yet."

"Okay, well I'm always here if you need someone to talk to," Megan said. "Do you need any help with dinner?"

"I would appreciate it if you both could bring the food into the dining room and it would be an immense help if you set the table while you're there."

"No problem," Nick said, glad to have something to add to the conversation. He scooped up the dishes and walked out toward the dining room.

Megan lingered behind and Marie handed her the steaming bowl of mashed potatoes. "There you go, and you can grab the rolls right there on the counter to bring out as well."

Megan held the bowl and stayed for a moment. "Marie, I know this is an awkward time to bring this up, but I had the distinct impression you wanted to tell me something the other night."

Marie held her gaze for a moment and said, "No, there's nothing for me to tell."

"Please, tell me if you know or saw something. Maybe that will be the key to getting these people out of here, especially if there's a killer living in Misty Manor."

Marie stared at Megan. Shades of indecision crossed her face as she considered telling her what she knew. She seemed ready to talk and then looked up and over Megan's shoulder. Savannah was standing near the doorway and behind her was Nick, coming back to the kitchen to see what else he could carry.

Marie's face blanched. She immediately turned around and took off her apron. "I'm sorry I can't eat with you all tonight, but I think I'd better get started on the laundry. I've got six bedrooms to make up each day. There are a lot of linens to be washed." Within seconds, she was gone.

Megan turned around to see Savannah head into the dining room. Walking up to Nick, she said, "I'm certain something has her scared. I think she was about to tell me, but I think she was scared off when she looked up and saw you."

Chapter Fifty-Six

"Megan, please come into the library," Teddy said as he stood at the solid rosewood door. It was Thursday morning and Teddy had finally returned.

Megan had been sitting in the parlor, sipping a cup of coffee and dreading this moment all night. She knew she was procrastinating. Not knowing whether she would have to leave the reading of the will and go upstairs to pack her bags, she tried to take in all the memories she could to form a lasting impression of her life inside Misty Manor. She didn't want to leave, but she didn't want to stay and watch her father destroy everything her grandmother had worked so hard to achieve. Megan had no idea what her father's plans were, especially now that Randall Douglas was dead, but she realized they wouldn't be to restore and preserve the Grand Victorian as it was many years ago.

Megan stood and took another moment to watch the ocean through the front window. She saw Georgie leave the house and begin her jog to the boardwalk.

Nick had stayed through dinner the night before, which was excellent if not subdued.

One by one, the guests had sauntered into the dining room and fixed themselves a plate. They initially appeared relaxed, but stiffened when they noticed Nick sitting at the table. Conversation was muted and very superficial when offered at all. Tensions were running high. Megan realized they were straining to be polite as long as the visitors from Texas weren't allowed to leave, but they were all becoming tired of each other's presence. A pressured strain hung over them like a cloud.

Midway through the meal, Georgie arrived at Misty Manor to stay the night. Her entrance seemed to lighten the mood. She grabbed a plate, announced she was starving and related tales of swimmers getting into trouble with high waves and rip tides throughout the day due to the impending rain.

Nick finished his meal, wiped his mouth with a napkin and announced he had to leave as he had unfinished paperwork at the station. The relief with his departure was palpable. Megan had to wonder why three innocent people, four, if you included her father, would be so worried when a police officer sat at the table. Someone had something to hide. That was for damn sure.

Once the guests had left the room, Megan and Georgie cleaned off the dining room table and brought the dishes back to the kitchen.

"Thank you for helping me, tonight," Megan said as she filled the sink with warm water and dish detergent.

"Hey, why don't you let me do those dishes," Georgie said as she threw another fork into the water.

"No, but thanks anyway. Tonight, may be my last opportunity to wash dishes at Misty Manor," Megan said.

Georgie looked concerned. "Do you really think so?"

Megan shrugged. "I have no idea. I guess we'll have to wait until tomorrow to find out."

"But Megan," Georgie persisted, "Do you really think your grandmother wouldn't have made provisions for you in the will? Secondly, do you really think your father would throw you out? He probably was just in a bad mood when he said that."

Megan shrugged. "Marie is acting weird too. I'm not sure if she knows something or not, but now that I think of it, my father may have issued some sort of warning. I know he's always been close to her, but Amber completely blew me away when she said she saw my father and Fran Stiles having drinks together. Can you imagine? That Stiles woman almost single handedly killed my grandmother while stealing her things."

"I don't know how to say this delicately, but the two of them are of the same ilk," Georgie said as she dried the last dish.

"My thoughts, exactly," Megan said as she drained the dish water from the sink.

Once the dishes were done, the pair bounced upstairs and got ready for the evening. They relaxed by playing music, reading magazines and freshening the room. They checked Megan's room and found the mattress was now dry and clean. The sheets and bedspread had been dried and folded. The linens being placed across the edge of the mattress in preparation for the bed to be made up.

The girls chose to stay in the room they were in the night before which afforded a better view in case additional visitors roamed the halls that night.

After several hours, they grew tired and soundly slept through the night, without noise from strangers outside their door.

Megan woke a few hours later, and unable to immediately fall back to sleep, began to entertain memories of her years at Misty Manor. She reviewed images of herself as a child playing on the beach, having dinner with Grandma Rose in the dining room, hiding in the attic, playing on the roof near the widow's walk, decorating the Grand Victorian during the holidays and hanging out at the lighthouse. Her stomach clenched with the thought she might have to leave tomorrow and never return to Misty Manor.

When the first rays of early morning light snuck in the room, Megan pulled the blankets over her and fell asleep for a full two hours. She was awoken by Georgie who was up and getting ready for a quick breakfast and her workday at the beach. Seeing Megan's hesitation to get out of bed, Georgie sat beside her to offer encouragement.

"Megan, everything will be fine. Have some faith in your grandmother and the big guy up above."

"I have no doubt when it comes to my grandmother's motives."

"But you aren't sure of others?" Georgie asked as she watched her friend.

"I'm naïve in that I assume all fathers love their little girls and all attorneys protect their clients, but what if Teddy and my father have some sort of secret deal going on? It's obvious I was wrong about the father assumption."

"Megan, you have no control over those things right now. You do have friends who love you and will be by your side to support you regardless of the outcome. If something isn't right, we'll help you find legal advice, but at this point, it is what it is."

Megan offered a small smile and squeezed Georgie's hand. "Thanks, I appreciate all you've done and for being here the last couple of nights."

"My pleasure. Thankfully, no one was creeping around here last night."

"I know," Megan agreed. "The only reason I want to get this day started is so we can get to the bottom of this whole mess and get these people out of here."

"Amen," Georgie said. "Anyway, I'm outta here. I'll definitely call you later tonight to see what happened, but in the meantime, keep the faith."

Megan was now in the parlor, listening to Teddy call her as she watched Georgie reach the boardwalk and picked up speed.

"Is everything okay?" Megan's head snapped up as she looked at Teddy watching her from the door.

"I'm sorry, so many memories are dancing in my head right now."

"I realize that," Teddy said, nodding his head. "But, everyone is waiting. Let's get started so we can get through this. It's bound to be emotional."

Megan's stomach dropped. She swallowed hard and walked toward the library. "Okay, let's get this over with."

Chapter Fifty-Seven

Megan walked into the library and was surprised to see several people sitting on one side of the table, a pile of paper and laptop in front of each. She didn't recognize anyone other than her father who was practically preening as he sat at the head of the table. Megan had to resist the urge to walk over and slap him.

Teddy guided her to a seat at the opposite end of the table, after which he sat in the empty chair next to his assistant, Ellen. Megan was certain they were not involved but was not positive. They certainly worked together showing polish and routine after many years.

As Teddy sat down, Ellen pulled out his glasses and arranged a few papers in front of him. She then went around the entire table and poured glasses of ice water for each person in attendance. When she sat down and placed the glasses dangling off a gold chain on her nose, Teddy thanked her and cleared his throat.

He looked around the table and began. "Thank you for coming today. We gather to mourn our dear friend, benefactor, mother and grandmother. Rose Stanford was a kind, gentle woman. She was also a woman of means, although she never flaunted her wealth. She used to say she was rich with love and the satisfaction she received when she performed charitable acts. Might I say, she was very generous, loved and satisfied."

Megan couldn't stop herself before she left out a sniffle. Her grandmother had been a wonderful woman and Megan really missed her.

Teddy paused and gave Megan a smile as Ellen brought her a small box of tissues. Teddy continued, "I have asked you all to be here today as the contents of Rose's will affects you all. To each of you, she has bequeathed a gift. I will read the will. Some of you will be asked to sign paperwork later and most of you will be asked to leave before the entire will has been read. There are some things Rose has requested to keep private. Is that agreed?" Teddy looked at the faces surrounding the table and all nodded in agreement. Megan continued to tear up as did some of the other women at the table. A few of the gentlemen looked sad. Her father, however, looked bored as he looked at his watch and crossed his right leg over his left knee.

"One more thing before I begin. Please silence your cell phone if you have one. There is to be no recording of the reading of Rose Stanford's last will and testament. If we catch anyone, you will forfeit your bequest and be removed from the premises. If any of this meeting finds its way to social media, you will be prosecuted to the full extent of the law."

"Is that understood?" Teddy watched as everyone nodded their assent. "I would ask each of you to go around the table and introduce yourselves to the other people present in the room. Some of you work on the same board of directors or committees. I would like to start by introducing Mr. Dean Stanford, the only son of Rose Stanford, on my right. On my left is Megan Stanford, the sole granddaughter of Rose Stanford. Will the rest of you please introduce yourselves?"

One by one, the other people in the room announced their name, their relationship with Rose Stanford and the charity, hospital or committee they were involved with. It amazed Megan to discover the extent of activities her grandmother supported. Her influence extended from local hospitals, to women's shelters, pet rescues and environmental committees. Once they were all properly introduced, Teddy turned his attention to the pile of papers and began.

"I, Rose Stanford, being of sound mind and body...," Teddy read as he turned pages in the will. He identified her legal representatives and the validity of the will.

As the sound of his voice continued, Megan drifted back to her thoughts and memories of her childhood once again. Images of her grandmother laughing and singing came to her and brought fresh tears and sadness. Megan refocused when she heard Teddy begin to name individual charities.

"To each of the following charities, I leave the sum of one million dollars to be used to benefit those in need." Teddy continued listing charities, directions and her wishes to continue their philanthropic efforts. Each representative nodded and smiled as they realized their causes had been funded for a while longer.

"Rose wanted to wish you each a final goodbye. Please look at the laptop nearest you." Teddy pushed a button on his computer and a video appeared. Megan's stomach clenched at the sight of her beautiful grandmother, sitting in her favorite peach damask chair in her bedroom. Her hair was drawn up and someone had applied makeup to her face. She looked lovely.

"Hello, if you are watching this video, I must be gone by now. Please don't cry for me as I believe I am probably in a better place. My goal has always been to spread as much love and kindness as possible, especially to those who are in need. I know you are champions of some of my favorite charities and I beg you to provide for the poor, the lonely, those that are ill and especially for any and all children who are in need. You are all kind, generous, brilliant people. I don't know what would be the best way to accomplish what you do, but I know you'll all figure out how you can accomplish remarkable things. In addition to my bequest, I challenge you to find ways to raise more money and make sure it reaches those who need it most. Be happy for me as I can bring love and joy in a new way. I will see you all again one day." Rose Stanford then blew a small kiss from her hand toward the camera.

Megan grabbed a small wad of tissues and sobbed for a few minutes as the visage of her grandmother opened a fresh wave of grief. The visitors near her comforted her by squeezing her upper arm and rubbing her hand.

Teddy put the paperwork down on the table. "I will pause here for now and take a moment to regroup."

"Do we have to?" Dean asked. "I'm good, let's just get this over with."

Teddy looked over at Dean and smiled. He then looked at the other people in the room. "At this point, the public portion of the will reading is over. I would ask you all to depart but to see Ellen on your way out and leave your most current contact information. We will be in touch soon."

Teddy then turned to Dean and Megan and said, "We will continue with the rest of the will in approximately twenty minutes." He turned toward Megan. "Please take a minute to refresh yourself and have a drink of water before we continue."

Megan's stomach knotted again. Teddy had to ask her to compose herself which may be his way of preparing her for shocking news. Megan stood up and left the room. Her head was spinning, her nose was stuffy from crying and she felt nauseous.

Blowing her nose, Megan made her way to the kitchen. She opened the refrigerator to check for some juice when she heard a voice behind her.

"Can I help you get anything?"

Megan jumped with surprise as she thought she was alone. She turned around to see Marie looking at her. She was holding a large pile of freshly folded linen and immediately placed it on the kitchen table when she saw Megan's face. "Here, let me make you a nice cup of tea." She busied herself by quickly pulling out a tea cup and heating water. She turned back to Megan and asked, "Guess it's not going too well in there?"

Megan shook her head. "I don't know. We haven't finished the reading yet. To be honest, I'm not supposed to talk about any of it."

"Well, I have to be honest," Marie said. "If you leave that room with your father owning any part of Misty Manor, I'm planning on walking out immediately. That's the reason I'm doing the linens for you now." Marie picked up the kettle and poured hot water over a tea bag. "And, just so you know, I also found out that your father had drinks with that scum Fran Stiles. I'm so angry, I'm spitting nails." Marie stirred a bit of sugar in Megan's tea and then added a small shot of brandy to the cup. She turned and handed the tea to Megan. "Here, this will help you get through the rest of the reading. Remember, the good Lord puts you where he wants you to be. There's no sense questioning what you get handed at this point. If we must leave Misty Manor, then it means we're being protected from a bigger mess down the line. You and your grandmother are survivors. That won't change today, just because of this."

Megan put her tea on the table and reached over to give Marie a hug. "You're right. I'll be fine either way. Thank you for all you've done for Misty Manor and for me."

"That's enough chit chat," Marie said as she pulled back. She picked up the tea and handed it back to Megan. "Go get 'em."

Chapter Fifty-Eight

Opening the library door with one hand, while balancing her tea with the other, Megan entered and resumed her place at the table. Teddy was still in his seat and was laughing at something her father had just said. Megan had not heard the comment but thought the two men looked chummy. Her father had obviously left the library and helped himself to a glass of scotch. Megan felt bad doubting Teddy's scruples, but she wasn't sure of anything, anymore. Either way, everyone was right. Just hear it out and move on, regardless of direction.

Teddy checked his watch and cleared his throat once again. "Okay, it's just family now. I'd like to take a moment to organize myself." Teddy spent a minute tapping the keys on his laptop before he announced he was ready. He looked up at the two of them and pushed a laptop in front of each. "For the next part, I'm going to ask you to watch a video. It'll be easier than reading from the document and Rose's wishes will be validated by her own words. I'll answer any questions you may have afterwards." Teddy checked to make sure each of their monitors were working and then went back to his own laptop and pushed a button. Within seconds, a video came to life and once again, Rose Stanford filled the screen. She was still seated in her favorite peach damask chair. Megan reminded herself to ask Teddy when this video was recorded. Her mind refocused when she heard her grandmother begin to speak.

"Hello, if things worked out the way I hoped, my son, Dean, and my granddaughter, Megan are watching this video in the presence of Teddy. The first thing I want to say is I love you both very much. It's been a year since Hurricane Sandy hit the coast of New Jersey and I could move back into Misty Manor. If the storm did anything, it proved how quickly things we take for granted in life can disappear. Sadly, that includes more than the material things we collect in our lives. Be that as it may, I'm having someone help me secure parts of

Misty Manor which were damaged in the storm as well as mobilize a special fund to help those in town who've lost friends, family or all their worldly possessions. Rebuilding and maintaining Misty Point will take some work and then oversight to ensure the work continues. I've had to strongly consider these things while making decisions about my affairs." Grandma Rose stopped for a moment and swallowed several times. She looked up and asked someone to give her minute.

The video feed went black for a moment but then popped back on and Rose seemed more settled. She smiled into the camera. "Okay, I promise I'll get through this. I'm getting good at this video business. I want to let you know what decisions I've made so you understand why I made the arrangements as I have." Once again, she resettled herself in her chair and continued.

"Dean, I've loved you forever. You were the most precious baby when you were born and I'm sorry you've had to grow up without your father. I don't know why or where he disappeared to and you were only five years old at the time. I guess I overcompensated and spoiled you a bit when you were young. I know you missed having a male influence while growing up and perhaps that's why you're always looking for the next important thing in life and to realize your full potential." Rose looked directly into the camera. "Dean, I tried my best and I'm sorry if I failed you in any way, but know I have always loved you. Misty Manor and the town will need someone to be their champion. Someone who is devoted and plans to live side by side with the people of the town." Rose paused, took a breath and looked directly into the camera. "Dean, we both know you were never happy here and that is exactly why I've decided not to leave Misty Manor or any part of Misty Point for you to worry about." Dean suddenly shot straight up in his chair, anger crossing his face as he continued to listen to the video. "I've released you from all obligations." Rose looked down at her lap and smiled. "Don't worry, I haven't forgotten about my son and I've advised Teddy to arrange for you to receive a sum of ten million dollars. He will place the money in a bank of your choice as soon as it can be arranged. I wish you much love, health and happiness and look forward to seeing you again, someday, in another place." Dean smiled and settled back in his chair, clearly satisfied with the amount of money his mother arranged for him.

Rose took a moment to take a sip of water from a glass which sat on a table situated next to her chair. She turned back to the camera and smiled. "My dearest Megan, my love for you has always been special as you are a remarkable, sensitive being. As you've heard, I've left bequests for my favorite charities, and a sizable sum for your father. The rest of my estate is yours. That includes all physical residual items such as Misty Manor as well as the assumption of all my appointments and responsibilities within my foundations and organizations. I know that all sounds rather scary, but Teddy will help you navigate the committees. You can decide which ones you'd like to work with and which you don't. Give it a chance, dear. You may be very surprised how much you can grow by helping others and I know you have the love and capacity in your heart to do so. But, if you decide not to continue, Teddy will turn control over to a selected representative and make sure they are funded appropriately. After that, Misty Manor, any residual property, all policies and accounts will still be yours. I will rely on Teddy to explain the significance of this arrangement to you." Megan's heart clenched as she realized she would inherit Misty Manor after all. Tears began to flow down her cheeks. She was frightened to step into her grandmother's shoes when it came to philanthropy and business, so she would certainly talk to Teddy. Megan wanted to beg him to remove her from that type of responsibility. She wouldn't be rich, but she would have Misty Manor and somehow, she would find the funds necessary to restore the Grand Victorian to its former beauty.

Megan looked up to see her father sitting in his chair, with a wry smile on his face. He was Rose's son, after all. He got what he wanted. A lot of money and zero responsibility and was quite happy about the arrangement.

Grandma Rose's voice made Megan refocus on the video. "Megan, I love you more than life itself and I can never describe the joy and happiness you brought to me as you grew up. I know you think I filled a void in your life, but what you don't realize is the void you filled in mine. I've thought a lot about our lives and I've left a few other things with Teddy to help you understand all my thoughts." Rose suddenly gulped and began to cry. Wiping tears from her face, she said, "I hope to see you once again and hold you before I pass on, but in case I never do, just know that the amount of love I have for you will last forever." Rose stopped speaking and waved to someone who was working the camera and the screen went black.

Megan inhaled deeply and began to sob. She was so glad she had come back to take care of Grandma Rose before her death, but still wished she had given her more of the seven years in between college and her return.

"I think that's enough for now," Teddy said as he turned off the monitors. He stood up and shook Dean's hand. "I will meet with you again later today or tomorrow. I'll ask you to provide your banking information at that time so we can settle your affairs. Thank you very much. I'd like to attend to Megan for a moment, alone, if I may."

"Sure," Dean said as he stood and picked up his scotch. He looked at Teddy. "I know you'll be able to explain to Megan that her inheritance still has value. If necessary, there must a few interesting items in the attic she can sell." With a smile on his face he strode from the room without stopping to comfort or congratulate his daughter.

Once he was gone, Teddy and Ellen both walked over to Megan who stood to greet them. They congratulated her and the trio hugged as a group. Ellen gave her a smile and said, "I'm so happy for you. Rose Stanford is smiling today. You'll bring life back to Misty Manor and that's what she always wanted."

"I'm sure going to try," Megan said. "I don't know if I'll have time to tend to the committees and such. I'll have to find a job, but I'll try my hardest to find the funds to restore Misty Manor, the way it should be."

Teddy frowned, then looked at Ellen and smiled. He took Megan by the arms and noted her hands were cold and trembling. "There is the one thing I didn't want to say in front of your father. Megan, look at me." When Megan looked directly into his eyes, he said, "Your total inheritance is worth approximately two hundred million dollars." Megan's face remained blank. Teddy waited a moment to let that sink in before he continued. "Your father is very pleased with himself as he thinks he has received a windfall. Maybe, one day in the future, someone will explain your worth to him in one of his social circles, but he won't be able to contest anything. Misty Manor, Misty Point and everything which goes along with it is yours. Rose had faith you would use your inheritance to do the right thing by the estate and those who surround it."

Teddy and Ellen continued to watch Megan as beads of sweat popped out on her forehead. Her eyes began to flutter upward. "Ellen, we better get her to the couch." They moved her over to the couch and placed her legs up on the arm rest so they would be higher than her heart. Ellen ran and placed cool water on a napkin and bathed her face.

Within a few minutes, the color returned to Megan's face and she sat up. She shook her head and swallowed hard.

"Are you okay, dear?" Ellen asked as she smoothed back her hair.

"Numb, I'm in total shock, but yes I'm pretty good," Megan said as she smiled.

Chapter Fifty-Nine

Teddy and Ellen straightened the library as Megan regained her composure. When ready, they opened the door. Megan walked them to the front door and outside onto the porch. She embraced them both.

"I'll set up a meeting with you as soon as possible," Teddy whispered into her ear. "We need to discuss banks and some official business but I think it best if we let a few things clear out of here. In the meantime, you have cash at the ready in your current account. I wouldn't announce anything much except that you are the new owner of Misty Manor. Congratulations again, Megan. Your inheritance is well deserved and we look forward to working with you and the foundation in the future if you'll have us."

"Of course, wow, yes, I'm still in shock," Megan said as she began to babble.

Laughing, Teddy and Ellen made their way off the porch and waved goodbye.

Megan turned and went back into the house. She felt nervous, but simultaneously wanted to shout, laugh, cry and run through the house screaming. Did that just happen or was she dreaming? She wanted to pinch herself. After all that, she felt bad about doubting Teddy. He was just trying to protect her from her father. Grandma Rose was still looking out for her. Maybe life could finally move forward.

Megan headed toward the stairs. She wanted to call Nick and needed her cell phone immediately. All the dread from the last day disappeared and she felt light as a feather. As she neared the base of the stairs, Marie came running out of the kitchen and embraced her. She was crying, but full of smiles.

"You heard?" Megan asked as she looked at Marie.

"Your father has announced to everyone that Misty Manor is now all yours."

Megan laughed. "And most definitely, not for sale. I have to call Nick and see when we can get these people out of here." Megan didn't notice the look that came over Marie's face as she bounded up the stairs. Instead Megan was wondering who had inherited Randall's life insurance.

Chapter Sixty

Reaching the bedroom, Megan flew over to her phone and called Nick. After three rings, she paced the floor saying, "C'mon Nick, please pick up." She was put through to his voice mail and left a message for him to call her as soon as he could. Megan then searched her contacts for Georgie. She dialed and waited for Georgie to pick up.

"Hello?"

"Georgie, it's me."

Alarmed at her voice, Georgie said, "Are you okay?"

Megan was so excited, she was breathless. "Georgie," she squeaked, "Misty Manor is mine."

"What?" Georgie shouted into the phone.

"Yes, I can't believe it." Megan began to elaborate when Nick's phone dialed in. "Georgie, I have to go. I'll talk to you later. We can celebrate." Without waiting for an answer, Megan ended the call and picked up Nick's.

"Hey, you okay?" Nick said. "I just saw the news and was worried about you."

"You heard already? It's on television? I can't believe how fast news travels around here."

"It was on television and social media. I think everyone in town saw it this morning," Nick said. "I was wondering what Abigail's reaction was, to be honest."

"I think she knows, but are we talking about the same thing?" Megan asked, realizing things weren't making sense.

"I don't know," Nick said. "What are you talking about?"

"Teddy just finished reading the will. Misty Manor is mine. My father blurted it out when he came out of the room, but I have the Manor."

"No kidding? Wow, that's great," Nick said. "I'm talking about the news your friend mentioned. They must have broken the story and now every major network picked it up. Like you said, bankruptcy and lawsuits over bad decisions and carcinogens in the last property. Does Abigail and Kevin know?"

"Oh, I have no idea," Megan said. "I've been in with Teddy all morning. Do you want me to see if I can find them?"

"No, do me a favor and stay where you are," Nick said. "I don't think this will go over well and it may be a catalyst to something worse, especially if they realize all the time they spent coming up to New Jersey was wasted as your father never owned Misty Manor to begin with. I'm on my way over. Please, don't do anything until I get there and assess the situation."

"Okay, I promise," Megan said. "Can I go to the kitchen and get a cup of coffee?"

"I guess that would be okay, but don't talk to anyone and if there's any sort of trouble, leave the house or lock yourself in your room."

"I promise," Megan said as she disconnected from the call. She took a few minutes to freshen up in the bathroom and change her clothes to something more comfortable from the morning meeting. Now starving, she made her way down to the kitchen for a cup of coffee and something to eat. She heard voices as she reached the bottom of the grand staircase.

"I can't believe this crap," Kevin yelled. He was in the parlor in front of one of the only televisions in the house. "Did you know about any of this?"

Megan approached the parlor and tried to peek inside to see who Kevin was yelling at. Abigail sat on the couch, her face was frozen in shock, and her complexion as pale as Megan's was an hour earlier. Kevin's cell phone was making all sorts of noises as calls and text messages were flying in, but for once he ignored them all. "I don't believe this. We're ruined. Douglas Development is ruined."

Abigail slowly shook her head from side to side as tears fell down her face.

Kevin continued to yell. "The company is already bankrupt. In addition, they're talking class action lawsuit and possible criminal charges. Several members of the board have already contacted their individual lawyers and are starting to make deals. I can't believe this. It's a good thing Randall is dead, because he wouldn't want to be anywhere near this black hole."

Megan backed away from the entrance to the parlor and silently made her way down the hall to the kitchen. She turned the corner in time to see Marie cooking at the stove and her father behind her, trying to place his hands around her waist. Marie turned around to face him with a knife in her hand and shook it in his face. "Don't touch me. I've spent years protecting you, defending you and believing that somewhere deep inside, you weren't the piece of garbage everyone saw you were. Well, that's over. Get away from me."

Dean laughed. "Marie, now we can finally have the life we always wanted. I'll have ten million dollars in my bank account within a few days. You can help me spend it. We can go to the Caribbean or Europe or wherever you want."

"Sure, until you see Fran Stiles or Gigi or some other floozy and take off for greener pastures. You've never had any respect or loyalty for women. I don't know what your problem is but if you don't back off, I'll use this knife."

"Marie," Megan shouted. "Not that I don't agree with you, but he isn't worth it. Put the knife down, please."

"You two are crazy," Dean said as he pulled the knife out of Marie's hand. Marie's face turned bright red and she made her way over to Megan who had come into the kitchen and was now standing on the side.

Marie began crying. Megan put her arm around her thin shoulders. "Is this what was bothering you? I know you've been keeping some secret the last few days. Was it something to do with my father?"

Marie's face went to stone and she said nothing.

"Please, Marie. You can tell me anything. Your secret may be the key to getting all these people out of here," Megan pleaded.

Marie continued to stare at the entrance to the kitchen. She then blurted out. "I did what you asked. I said nothing. Please don't hurt them."

Megan and Dean turned to find Savannah standing in the doorway. Her face was a mask of outrage. "Yes, you did. I'll give you that. But it doesn't matter anymore. Everything will come out now. It's over, all of it. And it's all your fault." She pointed at Dean. "You, for dragging our butts up here. Randall agreed not to look at any more properties and you kept at him until he left Europe and came to New Jersey."

Savannah then turned to Megan. "You had to keep asking questions, pushing buttons. Quite frankly, you've been a pain in the ass. I tried to warn you, but you kept going."

"You were the one who put the watermelon on my bed," Megan realized.

Savannah said sweetly, "I left you a note."

"Sure, along with a carving knife in my pillow," Megan countered.

Turning to Marie, Savannah said, "And you, my dear, just happened to be in the wrong place at the wrong time."

Marie bristled. "I was trying to accommodate a bunch of unwelcome guests. This isn't a hotel. If you had done what Nick told you and went to your rooms, there would have been nothing to witness."

Megan looked over at Marie with raised eyebrows.

"No one stayed in their rooms that night," Savannah said as she looked at Megan. "Don't be so high and mighty."

"I'm not," Megan protested. "I have no idea what's going on." She looked over at Marie. "Tell me."

Marie turned red as she spoke. "I was in the kitchen because I wanted to get a start on the cooking for the next day. Most of the alcohol had been moved into the kitchen and one by one everyone snuck down for more ice and another drink."

"Oh, really?" Megan asked.

"Abigail grabbed a bottle of scotch and a bucket of ice which she was planning on sharing with your father."

Megan made a face and looked over at her father.

"What? It was just a drink. Everyone needs to calm down around here." Dean shrugged as he spoke.

"What else, Marie?" Megan asked as she looked at her.

Marie looked at Savannah and stopped speaking.

Savannah's laugh was rich, deep and throaty. She shook her head. "It doesn't matter, anymore. My life is over anyway. What Miss Nosey saw was me pulling a special bottle of Bordeaux in a dark green bottle. We overheard that cop mention Randy had green glass in a wound on his head, she knew it was me." Savannah shook her head as she looked at Megan. "I told her if she opened her mouth I would kill everyone in this house, starting with you and ending with her so she could watch it all."

"Well she didn't tell anyone. I sure as hell couldn't get it out of her," Megan said as she turned back to Savannah. "Randy? I assume you two were close?"

"Close enough," Savannah said as she smiled.

Megan shook her head slowly. "So, then why did you kill him?"

Savannah's face turned dark red as she spoke. "It was an accident. I saw him come down from his room and I was trying to speak with him away from his wife." Savannah rolled her eyes as she continued to cry and sniff. She wiped her nose on the back of her hand and continued speaking. "I wanted to let him know about a serious problem. Right before we left to come to New Jersey, the office received a letter from a large attorney firm alerting us to the class action lawsuit."

Megan bit her lip as she listened. "And?"

"I wanted to tell him myself." She looked down and swallowed. "We were actually quite close over the last couple of years."

"You bitch," Abigail screamed out as she stepped into the kitchen. She had been out in the hall listening to the conversation with Kevin.

"Oh, please. If you weren't such an icicle, he wouldn't have needed to come to me."

Abigail raised her hand to slap Savannah, but it was caught by Kevin. "You don't need to do that."

Abigail turned on Kevin and laughed. "That's funny, because all this time, I was pretty sure she was screwing you."

"That was one time and apparently, a bad mistake," Savannah said, daggers coming from her eyes.

"Not my finest moment," Kevin said as he shrugged.

"Not that I want to interrupt, but I still don't understand why you killed Randall," Megan said.

"Yes, please enlighten us," Abigail said as she turned toward Savannah with her arms crossed. Savannah backed up so she was standing a few feet from the doorway with everyone else inside the kitchen.

Savannah took a deep breath. "I wanted to talk to him about the property, to tell him I was sorry."

"About what?" Abigail demanded.

"There was a report that came into the office from a special inspection right before we were scheduled to close on the last property. I didn't get a chance to open the envelope before we went to the closing. If I had, he would have seen the report on the possible presence of carcinogens and cancelled the deal, but by the time I read the report, it was too late. I didn't know what to do, so I shredded the report and prayed no one would ever find out."

"You what?" Kevin said, his face turning purple from rage.

"That's pretty much what Randy looked like when I told him," Savannah said as her faced reddened. "We were on the jetty. I told him I would help him fix things. I thought he would forgive me but he yelled at me. He freaked out and told me he was calling his lawyers, immediately. After all this time, I thought we meant something to each other. He didn't care how bad I felt. Then, he turned around to walk off the jetty. I was so mad and I had the bottle in my hand. The next thing I knew, I hit him over the back of the head with the bottle. I didn't plan to kill him, but he went down and hit his head on the rocks and rolled over into the ocean." Savannah swallowed a couple times while the rest of the group stared and was speechless. "I freaked out. I didn't know what to do so I returned and ran up to my room."

"I planned on leaving New Jersey and no one would know any better. But then, the officer saw the glass and started asking questions and I realized she knew I took the green bottle." Savannah pointed to Marie. She then turned to Megan. "And you, you wouldn't stop asking questions. I tried to shut you up."

"So that was you creeping around my bedroom the other night?" Megan said with an accusatory glare.

Savannah looked confused. "Sorry, honey. That wasn't me. I only left the warning note on your pillow."

"I am so confused," Marie said as she shook her head.

"Well, I think it's time we called the police," Abigail said as she began to stride toward the hall.

"Stop right there, bitch," Savannah said as she clenched her jaw.

The group stiffened as she pulled a gun out of the pocket of the hoodie she was wearing. She looked straight at Abigail and Kevin. "As far as I'm concerned you should all die but my last satisfaction will be taking you out with me."

"That's my gun," Abigail yelled.

"Yes, I searched your bags when you were drunk and took it for myself. You'd never use it anyway," Savannah laughed. "It's better that way, don't you think?"

"Do you really think you're going to get away with killing all of us?" Megan asked. "You better have a lot of bullets in that gun."

"Abigail brought quite a bit of ammunition," Savannah said as she smiled.

"What did you expect? After all, it's New Jersey." Abigail shrugged.

"I don't believe this," Megan said.

"Anyway, it'll be fun to see how many of you I get. As long as I save one for myself, no one will know exactly what happened."

In his most charming voice, Dean said, "Listen, no one has to get hurt today. Why don't you put the gun down? Shooting us isn't going to help anything."

"You know, I'm really kind of sick of you. You really think you can pretty talk your way out of everything, don't you?" A shadow crossed Savannah's face. "If you hadn't convinced Randall to fly to New Jersey, none of this would have happened."

Savannah aimed the gun at Dean's chest and fired. He managed to move fast enough to catch the bullet in his shoulder and fall to the floor, the knife clattering out of his hand.

Calmly Savannah laughed, looked at Megan and said, "Don't worry. I've got plenty more bullets."

Megan and Marie screamed and tried to run into the laundry room but Savannah turned and fired at them. The bullet hit the wall and stopped them in their tracks. "Don't move."

"Oh, crap," Kevin said as he back up toward the refrigerator, hands raised in the air.

Savannah turned to Abigail who began to tremble as she backed up toward the sink. "Please Savannah, put the gun down."

The group stared at the woman, her face half-crazed as she struggled with decision.

Megan looked up to see Nick and Chief Davis sneak into the kitchen. They were behind Savannah with their guns drawn and carefully watched her finger dance around the trigger.

"Drop the gun, now," Davis yelled as they started to fan out on either side of her.

Savannah turned and backed up toward the table where Dean was laying on the floor. His right hand was pressed against the wound in his left shoulder to curb the flow of blood.

"I said, drop the gun," Davis aimed directly at her. Static from the radio fastened to his vest announced reinforcements were on their way to Misty Manor.

Savannah didn't notice Nick had reached Megan and Marie and pushed them into the laundry room. Abigail and Kevin continued to watch, their faces filled with fear.

Savannah laughed as she stared at Davis. "We both know I'm not leaving here alive. I planned on shooting myself, but suicide by cop is just as good." Savannah raised the gun and pointed it directly at Davis.

Before she could pull the trigger, she let out a blood curdling scream and dropped to the floor. Davis ran over and kicked the gun away from her reach. Looking down, he realized Dean had plunged the knife into her calf while she was distracted.

Dean dropped back to the floor, extra blood squirting from his shoulder. Before he passed out, he managed to say, "Take that, you bitch."

Chapter Sixty-One

"Here's a cold one," Tommy said as he threw Nick an icy beer from the cooler. Megan and Nick were sitting in a circle of beach chairs accompanied by Georgie, Amber and Tommy. "You ladies want something to drink?"

Megan waved him off. She put her sunglasses on to watch the seagulls running near the water's edge.

"I'm good," Georgie said as she turned her face toward the sun.

"I can't have carbs." Amber adjusted the brim of her large hat to keep the sun off her face.

The group of friends had agreed to meet at the beach across from the Grand Victorian. They wanted to relax and blow off steam after a horrible week.

Three days had passed since Savannah Williams was arrested and pulled out of Misty Manor in handcuffs. She had been taken to the local hospital in the same ambulance as Dean. After being examined in the emergency room, Savannah was sent to the OR. The surgeon did his best to repair her lacerated tendon and muscle before sending her to recovery, her arm fastened to the side rail of the gurney with a pair of handcuffs.

Nick clinked his beer with Tommy and took a large pull of the icy liquid.

"So, I missed a lot of the fun," Tommy said. "Someone catch me up."

Nick looked over at Megan. She shook her head. "No, you start."

"Ok." Turning to Tommy, Nick said, "Well, you heard Savannah and Dean both went to the hospital, right?"

"Got that," Tommy said as he took a pull on his beer.

"Okay, Savannah was treated and remanded to a prison," Nick said as he turned back to Megan. Nick noted how the ocean breeze blew her hair across her face. Her lovely face which now contained a wide smile. "Your turn."

Megan pretended to frown. "Thanks. Alrighty then," Megan said, turning toward Tommy. "Poor Marie, once she stopped shaking, she spent the rest of the day cleaning the blood off the kitchen floor." Megan paused, she then turned and looked at the ocean, watching the seagulls hunt for food. She turned back and restarted. "My father is still in the hospital. He has to have surgery to correct the damage from the bullet in his shoulder. After that, he's scheduled to start rehab, but he's been on the phone with his ex-girlfriend, Gigi, every day. The minute she heard he'd been shot and inherited a lot of money, she decided to leave mom in Switzerland and call her man." The group chuckled at her description. "At any rate, he will not be coming back to Misty Manor."

"Cheers to Dad," Tommy said as he raised his beer in a mock salute. Amber giggled as Nick joined the salute.

"What about the rest of the group?" Amber asked. "Did they all go back?"

"Yes, they finally left," Megan said as she blew out a large breath. "A cab picked them up yesterday and brought them to Newark International Airport."

"Are you sure they left on the plane?" Georgie asked, picking up her sun screen.

"I didn't follow them to the airport," Megan said. "Once Nick told them they could leave, they were in such a hurry to get out of here I can't imagine they would stay any longer than necessary. It took an extra day for Abigail to make arrangements for Randall's body to be flown to Texas. I'm sure she wanted to be with him on the flight."

"What happens to her when she gets back to Texas?" Tommy asked.

"The company is a total mess," Megan said. "I feel bad for her. Once Savannah was out of the house and Nick said she could leave, she broke down and sobbed. She really had nothing to do with the company except her husband had some of the stock placed in her name. She'll start by burying her husband."

"And then what's left for her?" Amber asked, eyes wide.

"Nothing," Nick said. "Absolutely nothing but misery. Douglas Development will be dragged through the courts for many, many years to come."

"Do you think she'll face criminal charges?" Megan asked Nick.

"Probably not, but I'm not sure about Kevin Shaw," Nick said. "By now they've confiscated documents and computers to search through emails and such. It depends on what they find. Apparently, they both suspected each other of having something to do with the murder. Neither one of them knew who owned more stock in the company. With these problems, each one is hoping the other wins the contest."

Megan spoke up. "Before Abigail left, she told me she's the beneficiary of Randall's life insurance policy of one million dollars. If she gets to keep the money, she wants to use it to open a small antique store." Megan shook her head. "She'll have to do something to start over."

"That does seem to be a common theme," Georgie said as she offered her friend a bright smile. "So, speaking of starting over, what are your plans, my dear friend?"

Megan rubbed her arms and smiled. "I don't know. I haven't had time to think about it."

"Obviously, you're not leaving Misty Manor," Amber said. "Especially since you're the new owner."

"Cheers to the new mistress of Misty Manor," Tommy said as he raised his beer.

"Cheers," the group sang aloud.

Laughing, Megan said, "Yes, of course I'm staying at Misty Manor." She reached over and squeezed Nick's hand and received a squeeze in return. Megan had kept the rest of her inheritance a secret from everyone. She didn't ever want to wonder about their intentions or genuine friendship. "I would like to restore her to her former beauty."

"That sounds so cool," Amber said. "I'll help when I can."

"By doing what?" Georgie asked. "You may break a nail."

"I'm glad I didn't say that," Tommy said as he took another pull on his beer.

Amber scowled at one friend and looked back at the other. "Think about it, Megan. You could restore the house and make it a bed and breakfast."

"I don't know if I'm ready for that, yet," Megan said. "But once it's fixed up, it might be a lovely place to invite some distinguished guests."

Nick started laughing as he stood up and stretched. "Please do 'cause I'm tired of looking after your extinguished guests." He started to run toward the warm, salty water as Megan got up and chased him.

Georgie reached into the cooler and grabbed three cold beers. Offering one to Amber and Tommy, they clinked bottles, and smiled as she said, "To Rose. Thanks for bringing Megan home and keeping us together."

Other Works by Linda Rawlins

Misty Point Mystery Series:
Misty Manor
Misty Point

Rocky Meadow Mystery Series:
The Bench
Fatal Breach
Sacred Gold

About the Author:

Linda Rawlins is an American writer of mystery fiction best known for her Rocky Meadow mystery series, including The Bench, Fatal Breach and Sacred Gold. She loved to read as a child and started writing her first mystery novel in fifth grade. She then went on to study science, medicine and literature, eventually graduating medical school and establishing her career in medicine.

Linda Rawlins lives in New Jersey with her husband, her family and spoiled pets. She loves spending time at the beach as well as visiting the mountains of Vermont.

Made in the USA
Las Vegas, NV
22 February 2024

86134871R00132